THE
SUBSTITUTE
SAVIOR

SAM CAMPANELLI

Purple Baby Publishing
Williamsville, New York
Copyright 2013

To My Beautiful Mother~
Josephine Campanelli

Acknowledgements

Above all, I need to thank all the individuals that helped and encouraged me throughout the writing of this novel. As a Social Studies teacher of 23 years, I can say unequivocally that I am surrounded by the most talented, caring, and giving individuals you will ever come across in a profession. I could never have survived this journey without their guidance and assistance. The very first draft that I shared was with a dear friend and colleague of mine *Sue Calandra*. Sue was a bottomless well of encouragement, and she helped me to realize that what I was attempting was not a pipe-dream. Next, another friend and colleague with over 30 years of experience teaching, *Holly Morris*, graciously agreed to edit my next draft. Holly encouraged me to take the book to a higher level and was ultimately instrumental in guiding me to change the entire ending! One day, while doing some business as a union officer (GO WTA!), I mentioned I was writing a book to another colleague of mine, *Shaun Burke*. Shaun analyzed and edited the book, and helped me to see elements of the book from a fresh new perspective. The book cover art was created by; you guessed it, a colleague of mine in the field of art. *Annette Trabucco* took my vision of the cover and transformed it into exactly what I hoped it would be. The children of the Williamsville Central School District are truly blessed to have individuals like Sue, Holly, Shaun, and Annette teach them each day.

There are others I must express my gratitude towards. To be honest with all of you, I don't know if this novel I created is worthy of <u>any</u> praise in the literary world. I don't have any illusions that I am a "great writer". I am not a scholar in the field of literature; I'm a middle school social studies teacher who felt that there was a story inside of him that needed to be told. The best that I could hope from this novel is that the people who read it are touched emotionally by the characters and their life events. Yes, this is a book of fiction, but the universal attributes of love, compassion, sincerity, honesty, and spirituality are not fiction. These attributes have always been a part of my reality—thanks to my family. If you are wondering which parts of the book are based upon my life, seek out and recognize the goodness within many of the characters. When you find this goodness think of my beautiful mother (Josephine), my father and best friend (Donald), my wonderful wife (Christine), my three children, my brother and sister, my nieces and nephews, and of course, my dearest friends. I am blessed to have had all you in my life.

Yes, there is just one more group to thank—the nearly **3,000 students** I have taught in my career. If you are a former student of mine—yes, you are the inspiration for the students in my book! Notice how I portrayed many of the kids in the book—positive, insightful, intelligent, and caring. I certainly did not make that up. I did not need to because that is what I have taken away from all of you for over 23 years. To all my students—thank you for all you have given to me over the years.

Chapter 1

"Morning Mr. M. What's up?"

"Hey Mr. M. Are we gonna have homework tonight? *Please, please* don't give us any tonight. I'm sleeping over my Dad's house tonight, and he promised to take me to the hockey game."

"Mr. M, Uhhh, ummm … I kinda didn't have time to do my homework last night. I'm sorry. Are you mad?"

"Hi Mr. M. I'm having a *really* bad day today. Do you think I could go to the Guidance Office and talk to Mr. Corwin?"

"Hey Mr. M! We have our first game today. Coach said we had to wear a tie today. Do you like it?"

"Mr. M, I've been absent the last five days—did we do any work while I was gone?"

"Mr. Merriman, you look really tired today."

At age 41, Mr. Merriman had been teaching high school English in upstate New York for 19 years, and today, like most days, his students jump-started the day in typical fashion—an onslaught of greetings, excuses, messages, and questions. This daily practice of greeting each of his students was sometimes the best part of his day. Mr. Merriman's students could always count on seeing his silhouette posted outside of his classroom door at the end of the C-Wing hallway.

From the opposite end of the hallway, Mr. Merriman did not look very different from any other teacher in the hallway. It wasn't until you were about halfway down the hallway that you would begin to notice one of his most distinctive features—his stomach. Although Mr. Merriman was lean in the face, shoulders, arms and legs, his mid-section looked like he had swallowed a six-pound bowling ball. With a stomach so large it would be easy to label him as "fat", but that is not what came to mind when seeing him. This protruding stomach of his wasn't the result of layers of fat because it did not jiggle at all when he walked down the hall.

In fact, it just stood there taught and firm—like it was in suspended animation one foot in front of him. His stomach was such a source of intrigue among students that occasionally, a student would break the code of no physical contact between teacher and student and pat his stomach. Mr. Merriman would always pretend to be shocked when this happened, even though on the inside he was secretly laughing to himself. Later when asked, most students could not explain why they felt a need to pat his stomach. Their usual reply when questioned was, "I didn't plan on doing it. I didn't want to do it. I just couldn't stop myself!"

To the students who did not have him as a teacher, Mr. Merriman was just that odd teacher with the big stomach, who always wore short-sleeved dress shirts and a tie, and whistled every time he walked down the hallways. He probably didn't help matters because when students would ask him why he always whistled down the hallways, Mr. Merriman would simply reply, "Because it's the only instrument that I know how to play."

From three classrooms away, you could begin to see that he had a full head of hair and beard with about a sixty/forty percent ratio of gray to brown. Even though his hair seemed a little too long and messy for a man his age, his beard was always meticulously groomed. From this distance, Mr. Merriman seemed like an average looking guy—not too handsome, but not unattractive either. This opinion changed when you entered into Mr. Merriman's classroom though. One glimpse of his charismatic deep blue eyes and infectious smile, and suddenly he wasn't odd at all. In fact, he could even be considered handsome.

After all these years of teaching, Mr. Merriman still had a passion for his profession. Sure he had some days where he thought about retirement, and yes, it was getting more difficult each year to remember the names and faces of the thousands of students he taught over the years, but at this point in his career, he couldn't envision life without teaching. Wading through the waist deep pubescent amalgamation of personalities, moods, and life experiences of the 130 children he taught each day at Cayuga High kept him feeling young and alive.

Right from the start, he always knew that a desk or sales job was never going to do it for him. He had the necessary intelligence, talent and drive to compete for more lucrative jobs, but he was also grounded enough to know that the satisfaction of a large paycheck was fleeting. His salary of $65,000 a year was never going to get him a second home in Florida, but at least it left him with enough money to buy a Toro snow blower to clear his driveway of the lake-effect snows that came off Lake Erie each winter. His only "incentive bonus" was the front row seat he had to the always fascinating human interplay and drama at Cayuga.

It always seemed odd to him that most of the people he met responded with a hint of pity in their voices when he told them what he did for a living. He realized that many people would rather spend time in the Guantanamo Bay Detention Facility and be subjected to water-boarding than spend seven and a half hours a day teaching high school children. But to him, *they* were the suckers. He loved his job and most of them either hated theirs, or at the very least were indifferent towards them.

Mr. Merriman was the teacher that kids would later recall as being the teacher they would never forget—the person who most positively influenced their lives. The countless letters and chance meetings with former students out in the community all attested to this fact. He knew that many of his colleagues were more intelligent, more organized, and more learned than he was, but that never bothered him because he understood the simple secret to being a great teacher—"Let your actions and words always remind the children that you care about them and enjoy being with them. Do this and they will never forget you." This secret was an intangible part of all exceptional teachers' personalities, and for many, it cannot be taught—a person either had it or didn't. Well, Mr. Merriman had it.

In the near future, there would be one other reason why the students in his 8th period class would never forget him.

Chapter 2

"C'mon guys—stop screwing around! Let's just pick teams and play!"

"Sam and Mike, you be the captains—toss the bat to see who is going to pick first."

"Remember don't let the ball go into the Jackson's yard. If it goes into their yard again, Mrs. J. is going to kill us."

"Okay … Sam wins—you get first pick."

Ten-year old Samuel Amonte knew exactly whom he was going to pick first. In fact, everyone knew who he was going to pick first. Sam *always* chose the worse baseball player in the neighborhood—Kris Hawes. The other guys in the neighborhood couldn't understand why he always had to pick Kris first. However, Sam's best friend, Jimmy knew why—Sam did not want Kris's feelings to get hurt. If Sam was not selected as a captain, Kris was always picked last, and Sam couldn't stand to see the look on Kris's face when he was standing there alone in the hot sun waiting to be picked. In the adolescent world of the 1970's, that kind of sympathetic and empathetic nature could get you beaten up in Sam's tough city neighborhood. It was funny though; no one in the neighborhood ever dared to challenge Sam. Sure, they would tease him like the rest of the guys, but for some reason no one ever crossed the line with him. Jimmy could not recall Sam ever threatening someone or having to defend himself from any other kid in the neighborhood.

When Sam first moved into the neighborhood, Jimmy and Sam did not get along. It was probably more accurate to say that Jimmy did not get along with Sam. He felt threatened by Sam's arrival; Sam was tall, strong, and immediately became known as the best athlete in the neighborhood—a title that once belonged to Jimmy. Resentful of this, Jimmy used every opportunity to give

Sam a hard time. This went on for months, until one day in the heat of a football game; Jimmy went after Sam for tackling him hard at the end of the game. Jimmy simply "lost it", pushed Sam in the chest as hard as he could and stood nose to nose with him. Just before Jimmy was about to throw a punch, a weird thing happened; he looked into Sam's eyes and noticed that there was not a hint of fear, anger, or hatred. The only emotions he sensed in Sam's eyes were calmness and understanding. Sam put his left hand on Jimmy's wrist and without uttering a sound, seemed to communicate to Jimmy that he understood how he felt and meant him no harm. Instantly, Jimmy felt his anger drain away, and be replaced by embarrassment. To save face in front of the guys, Jimmy just pushed Sam away and stormed off the field. As Jimmy walked home, he could not understand how Sam knew what he was feeling at the time or how he could communicate it to him without a single word being spoken. From that day forward, Sam and Jimmy were best friends.

Jimmy was not the only one to recognize the uniqueness of his best friend. Anyone who met Sam could tell that he was different from the rest of the kids his age. The only person who didn't seem to notice it was Sam. For the first ten years of his life, he was oblivious to this difference. It wasn't until July 3, 1970, that Sam got his first hint.

Sam and all the guys from the neighborhood had gathered at the baseball field to play their daily summer baseball game. As they were picking teams for the game, Sam noticed a butterfly fluttering around Jacob Phister. At first, no one else noticed it. However, soon everyone noticed it because for some reason the butterfly kept trying to land on Jacob. A few of the guys began teasing Jacob.

"Hey Jake, maybe he thinks you are a flower?"

"Yeah, Jake—you know—because you are *soooo* pretty and sweet."

These comments bothered Jacob more than he wanted to admit, so he furiously tried to swat the insect with his baseball glove. After several flailing attempts, and more laughter from the guys, Jacob finally hit his target. Sam watched the butterfly hit the ground hard, struggle for a short while, and then begin dying in the hot sun. As Jacob was just about to step on it, Sam suddenly stopped him. Jacob called him a "sissy" and yelled for the guys to finish choosing sides, so they could start the game.

Sam, who was usually the best player on the field, was having an off day; he had already struck out twice and made two errors. He played the rest of the game, but could not seem to get the butterfly out of his mind. He kept looking over to the area where the butterfly lay dead in the hot sun.

After the game, when everyone went home for dinner, Sam lagged behind to go and look for the dead butterfly. When he found it, he saw that it had shriveled up to half its size. Sam reached down, carefully picked it up, laid it in his palm, and stared at it intently. He could not understand why Jacob had to kill this harmless, beautiful creature. He told himself to "get over it" and just go home for dinner. Just as he was about to drop it to the ground, the sun appeared from behind the clouds, and he was temporarily unable to see his hands through the intense light. As his eyes adjusted to the light, he looked into his hand and saw the butterfly move. Startled by this, he immediately dropped it to the ground. For a full minute, he stared down at the butterfly lying on the hot sidewalk, but it did not move again. As he reached down and gently cupped the butterfly in his hands for a second time—it suddenly moved again. However this time, he noticed that its' movement coincided with the feeling of a gentle breeze across his face. He knelt there feeling silly for thinking that the butterfly had suddenly "come back to life". It wasn't the first time that he let his imagination get the best of him.

"Samuel—dinner time!" his mother called out from their back porch five houses down from the baseball field.

"I'll be right there Ma!" he yelled back.

Sam rose to his feet and softly placed the butterfly into the grass near first base and ran to third to gather up his bat, ball, and glove.

As he ran across the field towards home, he spotted yet another butterfly dancing in the air just up ahead of him. He ran to it as fast as he could, but just as he got close, it flittered high into the sky above him. As it flew away from him he noticed that it looked like the same type of butterfly that he just had in his hand. He stood there in the field with his imagination front and center again, "Could it be the same one? No, it can't be. Let it alone. It's not the same butterfly. Go home!"

Instead of going home, he took several steps in the opposite direction towards the butterfly he had placed at first base. Once again, his mother called out to him. Hearing the stern tone in her voice, he stopped in his tracks and turned for home all the while looking back over his shoulder at the field.

When Sam arrived home his mother was in the kitchen preparing dinner. While she finished making dinner, he told his mother about the entire incident at the baseball field. As always, his mother sweetly indulged him by listening to his entire story from start to finish. When he was finally done, his mother simply said, "Of course it wasn't the same butterfly silly. Now, why don't you go upstairs and wash up for dinner?"

What his mother said next puzzled him, "By the way Sam, who was that old man standing beside you at the baseball field?"

Sam yelled, "What old man?" as he bounded into the living room to tell his father his story. As usual, he ended up cutting the story short because his father seemed more interested in listening to what Walter Cronkite had to say on television that evening than the events at the ball field that day.

Sam would never make it down to dinner that night. When his mother went upstairs to see what was taking him so long to get washed up for dinner, she found him in bed complaining about a sudden stomach-ache. As she bent over and pressed her cheek against his forehead, she noticed that he seemed a little warm. When she went down to tell her husband about Sam, he heard his father say that he was probably faking because they were having liver and onions for dinner. His mother knew her son was not faking that night.

Usually the early riser, Sam would stay in bed until 5 p.m. the next day.

Chapter 3

Like every student, every class of the day had a distinct personality to Mr. Merriman. One class was usually the "quiet and reserved class". This type of class was one where he had to slowly, over time, attempt to coax out their true personalities. Often this class was usually the first class of the day, probably because the kids had not fully woken up yet. Ask a question in this class, and he would only get a smattering of hands to go up. Students rarely *ever* spoke out of turn; they were compliant, focused and well-behaved. This type of class could learn in spite of him and required only minimal classroom management skills—it was every teacher's dream class. Mr. Merriman did not openly admit it, but every so often he secretly wanted them to be disruptive. Some days, he would purposefully try to create an atmosphere for them to be bad; unfortunately for him, they rarely took the bait.

Another type of class was at the total other end of the spectrum and was his most challenging class of the day. Most days, it would take at least five minutes to get them settled in and focused. Ask a question and everyone wanted to respond, and it did not seem to matter whether or not they had any clue as to what the answer was. Any small interruption in the lesson could send the class into a tailspin; a phone call from the main office, a pencil being sharpened, a late arriving student, or god forbid, any audible bodily function. He had to be at the top of his game to effectively teach this group of students. This was Mr. Merriman's great white whale, and he relished the challenge of teaching these students every day.

Mr. Merriman noticed that this type of class always seemed to fall immediately following lunch. For years, he could not figure out why; that was until he was assigned lunchroom supervision for the first time. Lunch period was the only unstructured time during the school day where kids were allowed to act "normal" and take full advantage of their *normalness*. As much as Mr. Merriman loved teaching, the one responsibility that he truly dreaded was lunch duty. Lunch duty had broken many a good teacher. Like the kids themselves, teachers took on totally different personalities while performing lunch duty. While patient, understanding, and sympathetic in their own classrooms, during lunch duty they took on the traits of every teacher they *disliked* when *they* were children in school. Oh, they tried to fool themselves each year that they weren't going to let the kids in lunch get to them. It was like the episode in *Seinfeld* where the character, upon coming out of an insane asylum, kept calm by slowly and quietly repeating the mantra, "*Serenity now, serenity now.*" For about a month, one could almost see the lips of the lunch duty teachers mouthing, "Serenity now, serenity now". However, just like in the *Seinfeld* episode, the mantra ultimately failed and the teachers' bottled up emotions eventually exploded. By October, lunch duty teachers were demanding that students get on their hands and knees to pick up every crumb within a ten foot radius—every student was guilty, none were innocent. Sesame-seed bagel sandwich day was the most stressful lunch of them all. No child's education would continue on that day until every sesame seed was picked up from the lunchroom floor. In short, at lunch, children's personalities blossomed and teachers' wilted.

Mr. Merriman's 8th period class, his last class, was the third type of class, and it was his favorite of the day. The best word to describe the atmosphere in this class was "connectedness". From the very first day of school, there was a special feeling in the room. When he spoke to them, they seemed to hang on his every word. Every day he found himself opening up more and more to them. As his students began to trust him more, they in turn opened up as well. It was an ideal atmosphere for learning not only English lessons, but life lessons as well.

When he first started teaching, he made the mistake of trying to make sure that he acted the way a teacher should act. It was very easy for new teachers to settle into playing "the role". He quickly found himself becoming a composite of the many teachers he had had in school and what school administrators expected "good" teachers to act like. Even though schools are designed to act as agents of socialization for students, they also worked to socialize teachers as well. Teachers are expected to be prompt, prepared, efficient, organized, compliant, all knowing in their subject area, and have the ability to work and get along with anyone. In short, they are expected to be the perfect role models. Sometimes in an effort to mask any "shortcomings", teachers will hide behind "the role", rather than simply be themselves. He witnessed many teachers spend their entire careers that way and never really open themselves up to their students. After spending several years like that, Mr. Merriman realized he was cheating not only his students, but himself as well. He decided he was not going to be just another actor on the educational stage. He came to learn that the more sincere and truthful he was with himself and his students, the more his students connected with him. He thought, since no child is perfect and shouldn't be expected to, why spend the whole day trying to appear flawless in front of them? So, little by little, over time, Mr. Merriman became more and more comfortable being himself in front of his students until he finally reached the point where he was able to approach each class in the same way—"This is who I am; accept me for all that I am, and I will accept you for all that you are. None of us is perfect, so let's come together every day and work on becoming better people together."

Mr. Merriman felt closer to his eighth period class than any other class he had taught in his career. This unique group of children needed him to be more than just a teacher; he had to be part father, mentor, psychologist, and friend all in one. In fact, it seemed to him that he spent as much time in the other roles as he did— "the teacher". Some of the students only needed a good teacher. Some needed a father figure. Some needed a strong role model. Some just needed someone to listen to them. Others struggled with deeper emotional and psychological issues. A few needed Mr. Merriman to utilize *every one* of his roles when he interacted with them. As this was his last class of the day, Mr. Merriman was usually pretty tired when his 8th period class walked through the door; yet these kids always seemed to find a way to energize him as the period went on. One day, however, for some reason, as the class went on Mr. Merriman just could not seem to muster his usual energy.

Chapter 4

  Sam had never been very close with his father. Although his father was a good man, provider, and husband, he always seemed to be closed off emotionally. Although he rarely yelled and never showed any violent tendencies—he clearly came across as being a resentful man. When he mentioned these things to his mother, she tried to reassure him by saying that it wasn't Sam's fault and he shouldn't take it personally. She usually ended conversations like this with, "Your father was like that from the day I met him and will probably always be like that, but I love him dearly and you should too." Sam did love his father, and his mother's words were usually enough to make him feel better, at least when he was younger. But as Sam became a teenager, her words didn't seem to help anymore because it was clear to him that his father did have a problem with him, and he could pinpoint the exact night when that became crystal clear.

  Sam and his father were coming home late one night from visiting his grandmother. He loved and hated visiting his grandmother. When he visited her, she was always so excited to see him. She always had a gift waiting for him and spent the entire time just plain spoiling him. While he loved being treated this way, the thing that he loved most was the time he and his grandmother would spend sitting and talking in her garden. Sam could sit there for hours listening to the stories about his father as a young boy and the grandfather he never met. The only thing he knew about his grandfather came directly from his grandmother—his father never spoke of him. The only picture he had ever seen of his grandfather was a black and white wedding picture from the 1920's that his grandmother had on display in her living room. His grandmother always told Sam how much he reminded her of his grandfather. Whenever they talked about his grandfather, his grandmother always ended the conversation with tears welled up in her eyes and gently placing her hand on his heart saying, "Sam, you have the same beautiful soul as your grandfather." Sam's visits with his grandmother were special for one other reason as well; it was the only time he ever saw his father show genuine affection and love towards another human being other than his mother. While it was never an overt display, he could see it in his father's eyes and the subtle, loving way in which he touched her.

Unfortunately, there was still the one thing he dreaded about these visits—the way in which the visits usually ended. Invariably, at some point, his grandmother would bring up the subject of his grandfather in front of his father. Almost immediately, Sam would see his father become agitated. It always hurt Sam to see that look of love and affection immediately vanish from his father's eyes at the mention of his grandfather. So many questions would flood into Sam's head when this happened. How could his father hate his own father so much? What did his father do to him to make him feel that way? If his grandmother said he reminded her of his grandfather, and his father hated him so much, where did that leave Sam in his father's eyes? As usual, his father became angry, grabbed his arm and pulled him out to the car to leave. As he sat in the front seat and looked at this grandmother in the kitchen window, he thought to himself, "Why did she have to mention his grandfather again and ruin the visit?"

Sam and his father had been driving for about 20 minutes in total silence on this particular night when he finally summoned the courage to ask about his grandfather.

"Dad, why do you hate your father so much?"

His father just continued to drive into the night without a response.

A few moments later, Sam said, "Grandma always talks about what a special person he was—she even says that I remind her of him."

Sam's father immediately shot him a look of anger and yelled, "You are not like your grandfather—you are nothing like him!"

Just then, Sam felt the car swerve violently. As he took his eyes off his father and looked forward, he saw the front windshield shatter. The next thing he knew, the car had come to a screeching halt in the middle of the road. His father was shaken and sat there for a moment tightly gripping the steering wheel with his forehead pressed against the back of his hands.

Upon gaining his composure, his father took his hands off the wheel and ran his hands over Sam's body in an effort to see if he was injured. Sam reassured his father that he was okay. Sam asked his father if he was okay, but his father just opened the door and started walking towards the back of the car and down the road. As his father walked away, Sam looked out the back window and spotted something lying on the ground about ten feet ahead of his father just on the side of the road. Sam opened his door and apprehensively walked back towards the figure on the ground. As he drew closer, Sam could see that it was a young doe.

Sam had never seen an animal so badly injured before. Its body lay there twisted in an unnatural position; two of the doe's legs were broken, and Sam could see blood coming from its mouth and ears. At first, the animal's breathing was labored, but as Sam continued to watch, he noticed the breathing began to rapidly slow until it finally stopped. Sam felt his knees start to buckle, and if his father did not grab him by the collar, he would have hit the ground hard. His father carried him over to the side of the road and told him to stay seated while he attempted to flag down a passing car for help. As Sam's nausea began to subside, he slowly crawled to the animal and laid his hands and face on its neck and began to cry. While he was crying, he heard his father yelling to get away from the deer and go back to the side of the road. Sam unsteadily rose to his feet and began to move away from the deer. However, Sam was so overwhelmed with pity and sorrow that he rushed back to the deer. Back on his knees, with his hands upon the deer, Sam felt himself moving between what seemed like a dream and reality. Suddenly, a bright light from behind him lit up the scene before him. At first, he assumed it was from an on-coming car, but he did not hear the sound of an engine because the road was quiet and desolate. Just as he was about to look behind him to find out the source of the light, he felt a hand grasp his shoulder, and say in a calm, quiet voice, "You can help her Sam."

Sam shaded his eyes to see who was talking to him, but could only make out the outline of a small, older man. Again the figure spoke, "Help her Sam."

Sam began to feel a commanding confidence come over him. Although the animal was not breathing anymore, he could still sense a faint presence of life in its body. He adjusted his body so that his head was now resting near to the doe's heart and his arms were clutching her chest. Sam could sense everything that was wrong with the animal. He could literally feel the pain of the animal within his own body. Mentally, he concentrated upon an image of the animal rising up off the ground and bounding into the woods. He kept playing that scene over and over in his mind for several minutes. It was then that he began to feel the first faint beat of the animal's heart.

"Thump."

Then quickly there was another—only much stronger this time, "Thump-thump."

Soon, the doe's heart was beating strong and regular. Sam could sense a feeling of strength and power surge through the animal's body. He could hear the blood rushing from the heart throughout the body. The body that had become limp was now becoming tense and taught. Strangely, as the animal grew stronger, Sam began to feel weaker.

What happened next was something that Sam could neither believe nor explain. The doe that was once crippled and dead was now beginning to push off the weight of Sam's body. At

21

first, there were several sudden spasm-like movements. Then in an instant, the animal threw Sam's body completely aside. He was thrown off so forcefully that he found himself flat on his back on the side of the road. When Sam stumbled back on to his knees, he had to close his eyes several times to make sure what he was seeing was real. The doe was standing up on all fours. She stared at Sam for several moments with eyes as big as her ears, licked the tip of her nose with her tongue, and then bounded off into the dark forest. Sam just knelt there stunned.

When Sam finally got a hold of himself, he immediately looked up to see if his father had seen this event. When he spotted his father, he was about twenty yards ahead of their car on the other side of the road. He was leaning into the window of a passerby who had stopped to help. Sam called out to his father as another car passed by. When his father finally looked back, he motioned to Sam to stay where he was.

The driver who had stopped to help his father, pulled past their car, did a u-turn, then pulled up behind their car and bathed the scene of the accident in light. Sam's father, who had now crossed back over the street, was walking back to the scene.

As he walked closer to Sam, his father's gait suddenly began to slow, until he finally stopped with a look of bewilderment on his face. Sam tried to tell his father what happened, but his father cut him off and said, "Sam … where is the deer?"

Sam started to explain, but was interrupted when the man from the car walked up and said to Sam's father,

"Hey man, I thought you said that you hit a deer?"

His father started nervously walking back and forth along the roadside searching for the dead animal. Sam once again tried to speak, but his father just kept searching back and forth without acknowledging him. The man who stopped to help said, "Listen man, if you guys are okay, I am going to take off. Are you sure you can drive?"

With his eyes frantically searching for the deer, Mr. Amonte responded, "Yes, right, I'm good. Thanks."

Finally, Mr. Amonte stopped searching, looked Sam straight in the eyes and said, "Where is the deer?"

Dad—I've been trying to tell you—I helped it."

What do you mean you *helped* it?"

Sam said, "It's back in the woods."

Sam's father responded tersely, "You mean you dragged it into the woods by yourself?"

"No", Sam responded, "she was dying, and I made her better."

Mr. Amonte was growing more and more agitated with each response. Finally, he shouted at Sam, "What are you talking about? What did you do with the deer?"

This time Sam looked his father squarely in the eyes and said, "Dad ... her heart stopped beating, and I made it beat again. She ran off into the woods ... on her own."

Sam's father grabbed him by the shoulders and pulled him forcefully towards him.

"Sam stop talking nonsense! Stop lying to me! Where is it?"

With tears streaming down his eyes, Sam looked up at his father and quietly said, "Dad ... I saved her."

Mr. Amonte slowly loosened his grip on his son and backed away, looking as if he were lost in a distant memory. Sam took several steps towards him, but his father just backed away as if he was repulsed by the idea of Sam being near him.

Sam went back to the car and waited while his father searched the edge of the forest for nearly an hour. When his father finally crawled back into the car, he was covered with dirt, leaves, and sweat. Sam tried to talk to his father several times on the way home, but his father acted as though he was not even in the car. Sam felt his body growing weaker with each silent mile that passed.

When his mother heard the screen door slam, she hurried into the kitchen to see why they were so late.

"Anthony ... Sam—where have you guys been? I called your mother's house, and she said that you left over two hours ago. What happened? Your clothes are filthy, Anthony. Oh my God, Sam! Are you bleeding?"

She was visibly shaken at seeing the condition of her husband and son. In order to calm her down, Mr. Amonte explained to her that they had hit a deer on the way home; the blood on Sam was from the deer, and assured her that both of them were okay.

When Mrs. Amonte finally calmed down, she practically had to carry Sam upstairs to the bathroom to change out of his bloody clothes and wash the blood from his body. Sam took off his clothes in the bathroom until he was down to just his underwear. Mrs. Amonte wet down a washcloth with warm water and began to wipe the deer's blood from his body. It took a good twenty minutes to get his arms, chest, and neck clean. Sam's face was splattered with blood, too, so she went on to washing his face as well. When she was finished cleaning Sam's face, she wet down a fresh washcloth to go over his body for a final rinse. However, when she turned back to him, she spotted a little more blood around his nose and ears. Even though his mother thought she had wiped his face thoroughly of the blood the first time, when she attempted it a second time, she suddenly realized that this was not blood from the deer; it was Sam's own blood that was coming from his nose and ears. She picked up another washcloth and instructed him to pinch his nose with it, while she pressed the other to his ear.

She called out to her husband, "Anthony! Get up here now; he is bleeding!"

His father hurried upstairs to the bathroom and pulled the washcloth away from Sam's ear. He saw that Sam was indeed bleeding and said, "I don't understand this, he had his seatbelt on.

I didn't see him hit his head at all. He said he was fine and didn't get hurt."

Mrs. Amonte pleaded with her husband, "Anthony, we have to bring him to the emergency room! Something must have happened; he is bleeding from the nose and ears."

They spent nearly six hours in the hospital emergency room that night. Even though a battery of tests was performed on Sam, none of the physicians were able to explain the bleeding that had occurred from Sam's ears. He was eventually cleared by the physicians to return home that same night with instructions for them keep a close eye on him and call if they noticed more bleeding. His mother checked on him every hour on the hour that night; however, no more bleeding had occurred.

Sam did not awaken until 7:00 p.m. the next evening. When he finally woke up, he came downstairs and told his parents that he felt fine and was very hungry. However, even though Sam may have felt fine physically, he was not feeling well mentally. Emotionally, Sam was confused and frightened by the events of the previous night. After he was finished with dinner, Sam went out to sit on the front porch and watched the cars go by and the neighborhood children play under the streetlights. As he slowly rocked back and forth in the old metal porch chair, he realized that he felt lonelier than he had ever felt in his life. Watching the kids play under the streetlights, he felt terribly disconnected from them. How could they or anyone possibly understand that the night before he had brought a living organism back to life?

Chapter 5

As 8th period rolled around, Mr. Merriman stood posted at his door as usual, and of course, had something to say to each of his students.

"Good afternoon. Are you ready to learn today Olivia? ...That's the answer I want to hear!"

"No homework tonight, Mason. Have fun with your Dad at the hockey game tonight."

You don't have your homework, Jenna? I called your house last night, and no one answered. I just assumed that you were too busy doing my homework to answer the phone...I guess I was wrong about that."

"What's wrong Alexandra? Oh, you are *not* going to walk into my classroom without a smile today! ...That's better. Sure, you can go to guidance and see Mr. Corwin."

"Love the tie Alex. Did you tie it all by yourself? ... Next time, just ask Mr. Massina if you can borrow one of his clip-ons."

"He's alive! You were on vacation Daequan? Wasn't ten days off during winter recess enough? Was that essay on *To Kill a Mockingbird* so difficult that you needed five days on the beach in Florida to recuperate?... Don't worry, you didn't miss anything those five days—we just partied most of the time."

"Don't worry Clare; I'm okay—just a little under the weather."

The last student to usually enter the room was a 15 year-old young man named, Andrew Lambert. Mr. Merriman always made the biggest deal when Andrew came into the classroom. However, not one student was the slightest bit jealous of the attention Mr. Merriman poured on Andrew each day. Mr. Merriman was in rare form on this day.

"Lambert!" he shouted down the hallway. "You're going to be late!"

At that moment you could hear just about every classroom door in the C-Wing close. Every door except Miss Petrucci's—she loved to watch this daily ritual.

"Lambert—how come you are always the last one to get to class?"

All the kids in his classroom watched him standing outside of his door hands on his hips, back arched, and his stomach protruding forward.

"I know what you were doing …You were flirting with the 9th grade girls again! Give them a break Lambert; they can't concentrate as it is in class. Now they are going to be thinking about your ripped pecs and biceps all math class." The entire class at that point erupted into laughter.

"Are you kidding me Lambert?" Mr. Merriman now looked into the classroom and said to the class, "My Goodness! Andrew 'pimped' his ride!"

Just then, Andrew came through the door with huge smile on his face, riding a brand new candy apple red, motorized, wheelchair. The entire class got out of their seats and rushed over to Andrew to gush over his new "wheels". If Andrew wasn't strapped into his chair, his entire body would have floated off the wheelchair from the attention he received from Mr. Merriman and the kids in class. Colleen O'Brien, Andrew's educational aide, who was responsible for taking care of his many needs in school, stood there with Mr. Merriman smiling at all the fuss the kids were making over Andrew's new wheelchair.

After about five minutes, Mr. Merriman said to the class, "Okay, okay. If you guys keep this up, Andrew's head is going to get so big that he is going to have to buy an even more powerful wheelchair to get around with. Let's get to work people."

One by one, the kids filtered back to their seats, while Mrs. O'Brien settled Andrew into his desk at the back of the room. Mr. Merriman instructed the class to get out their copies of *To Kill a Mockingbird* and walked to the back of the room to get his copy from his desk. When he walked past Andrew's chair, Andrew reached out his hand and clumsily grabbed at Mr. Merriman's hand. Mr. Merriman looked down at Andrew's contorted hand holding on to his and smiled. But as he went to continue on to his desk, Andrew gripped his hand tighter and spun him around. With all the strength he could muster, Andrew pulled Mr. Merriman down to eye level. When Mr. Merriman looked at Andrew's face, he noticed it was intensely serious, and tears were welled up in his eyes. When Andrew knew he had Mr. Merriman's full attention, he whispered to him, "You're the man, Mr. Merriman."

For the first time in his career Mr. Merriman was at a loss for words. As he began to walk away, Andrew added, "Hey Mr. M, don't let your head get *too* big."

As he walked away from Andrew's desk, Mrs. O'Brien could see a reflection of Mr. Merriman in the back window near his desk. Just as he got there, he turned his face away from the class and seemed to wipe a tear away with the back of his hand. Soon after, Mr. Merriman shouted, "Let's get this party started—everyone turn to page 114 in your books; we have some quotes to analyze!"

Chapter 6

Many years had passed since the night of the car accident with the deer. Although Sam had never been particularly close with his father before the accident, Sam found himself at age 16 wishing he could turn back time and go back to the way things used to be between his father and himself. Since the night of the accident, the relationship between them had grown even more distant. His father now only seemed to talk to him when he had to. He wanted desperately to be able to sit down with his father and talk about what happened that night and the feelings and thoughts that were constantly running through his mind. However, for reasons unknown to Sam, his father's reaction that night and his subsequent actions, sent a clear message to him that what had occurred on that night was horribly wrong. Even though several opportunities arose during this time period to repeat the "power" that was mysteriously bestowed upon him, Sam turned his back on them because he could not stand the thought of further alienating his father. However, the tragic events of June 1, 1985, forced Sam to finally choose between his gift and his relationship with his father.

On this day, Sam, now a senior in high school and his American Legion baseball team, the Braves, were playing for the county championship against the Yankees. Many of his friends from the neighborhood were playing in the game, including Jimmy, who was the starting pitcher for the Yankees. They both knew with graduation approaching that this could be the last time they ever played ball together. They playfully taunted each other days before the game, with Jimmy saying he was going to "dust off" Sam if he crowded the plate, and Sam saying was going to point to the exact spot where he was going to hit a homerun off of Jimmy.

Just before the start of the game, Jimmy and Sam, the captains of their teams, met at home plate with their coaches and the umpires to go over the ground rules for the game. When Sam and Jimmy shook hands, Jimmy gestured down to home plate and said to Sam, "That's mine; don't get too friendly with it."

Sam responded by pointing to a tall sunflower over the right field fence and said, "After I knock the seeds off that flower with my homerun shot, I'll share a few with you after our win."

Both boys smiled and headed back to their benches. Sam spotted his father and mother sitting on lawn chairs along the right field line and saw his mother point her index finger to the sky and twirl it in a circular motion—a signal to Sam to hit a homerun for her. Sam shot her a quick smile.

The championship game was classic baseball—exceptional pitching and flawless team defense. By the last inning, a light rain had begun to fall and the score was tied 0-0. Jimmy had all his "stuff" on this day—his curve, slider, and fastball. It was the best game Sam had ever seen Jimmy pitch. Jimmy had already struck out ten batters, and the best the Braves could muster were weak groundballs to the infielders. Although deep down he was happy for Jimmy, Sam wanted to win this game badly. With one out in the bottom of the last inning, Sam came up to bat and purposely crowded the plate. This did not go unnoticed by Jimmy because he threw a high, hard fastball that forced Sam to bend over backwards and fall to the ground. Upon getting up from the ground, Sam brushed the mud off his hands, smirked at Jimmy, and pointed to the sunflower in right field. With the next pitch, Jimmy made his first bad pitch of the game and hung a high curveball over the plate. Sam jumped all over it, and sent it deep into right field. For a moment, Sam thought it was a homerun, but when he saw it bounce off the top of the fence back into the field, he sprinted to second for a stand up double. Sam looked at his Mom, and she raised her palms to the sky and shrugged her shoulders as if to say, "What—just a double!" Sam could not help but laugh to himself.

As Sam stood on second base and the rain began to fall harder, Sam saw his coach give the next batter the sacrifice bunt sign, which meant that Sam would have to run as fast as possible to third upon contact. His teammate executed the bunt perfectly. Now Sam was on third, and the Braves were one hit away from the league championship.

With two outs, Sam knew he was going to have to run hard on any ball that was hit. When he looked up to see who the next batter was, he realized that it was Kris Hawes. He noticed that most of the guys on the bench were looking down at their feet dejectedly because the worst hitter on the team was now up to bat. Kris's expression was even worse; he looked like he wanted to be anywhere in the world but the batter's box. Sam started clapping his hands, cheering Kris on and reassuring him that he could do it.

The first pitch Jimmy threw was a fastball right down the middle. Kris didn't even lift the bat off his shoulder—he just watched the ball go right into the catcher's glove. Sam said, "C'mon, Kris ...You've gotta swing the bat. You can do it!"

The next pitch was another fastball and this time Kris took a swing at the ball, but was a full second and a half late. Sam's coach called a time out and called Kris over to the third base side with Sam joining them. Although the coach was instructing Kris to be ready for another fastball and to swing earlier, Sam interrupted and told Kris and the coach that he knew exactly what Jimmy was going to throw on the next pitch—a slow change-up. Coach asked him if he was sure, and Sam convinced him that after years of playing ball with Jimmy, he knew what pitch was coming next. Before Kris went back to the batter's box, Sam grabbed Kris's arm and said, "You have to be patient—wait on the pitch. Now, bring me home!" Kris nodded and gripped the bat tightly as he walked towards home plate.

Sam took a huge lead off third and watched Jimmy as he went into his wind up. He could tell immediately by Jimmy's arm motion that his prediction was correct—a slow change was on its way. It seemed like an eternity for the ball to reach home plate, but when it did, Sam heard the greatest sound he had ever heard in his life; the sound of bat on ball. When Sam looked up, he saw that the ball was hit hard and heading straight back towards the pitcher's mound. Sam just put his head down, pumped his legs, and slid hard into home. Intertwined with the catcher, Sam looked up from the ground, and saw his entire bench erupt in celebration.

Sam jumped from the ground, threw up his arms and looked back to see what had happened on the field. When he turned back towards the pitcher's mound, he saw Jimmy lying on the ground with the ball two feet away. As teammates mobbed Kris and Sam, Sam realized that Jimmy was not moving, and parents, players, and coaches were running over to him with concerned looks on their faces. Sam pulled himself away from the rest of the players and raced over to Jimmy. At first, adults were yelling at players to move away; then they were yelling for someone to call an ambulance. Jimmy's mother was on the field screaming, "He's not breathing! He's not breathing! Please someone, do something!"

When Jimmy threw the pitch, he did not expect Kris to make contact; because of this, Jimmy did not get his glove up in time to react. The hard hit ball struck Jimmy in the chest with such force that his heart stopped beating.

Kris's father, who was a physician, performed CPR on Jimmy for almost fifteen minutes until the paramedics arrived. Everyone watched in horror and disbelief as the paramedics did everything they could for him. When the paramedics suddenly stopped working on Jimmy, everyone realized that the unbelievable had just happened.

The events of the last half-hour passed by in a confusing blur for Sam; but when he saw Jimmy's body being placed on the stretcher, time suddenly slowed to a crawl. *"This was not happening...Jimmy is not dead...He cannot be taken from this earth."* Sam began to chase after the paramedics as they wheeled

Jimmy to the ambulance. His father tried to stop him, but Sam tore free and began shouting at them to stop. Sam grabbed one of the paramedics arm and shouted, "Don't take him away, I can save him—I can save him!" Mr. Amonte came up behind Sam and grabbed him tightly around the arms to stop him. Sam pleaded with him to let him go as the paramedics now lifted Jimmy's body into the back of the ambulance. Despite his father's strength and size, Sam was able to wrestle himself from his grasp.

After loading Jimmy into the back of the ambulance and closing the doors, the paramedics walked to the front of the ambulance to rush Jimmy to the hospital, but Jimmy's mother grabbed one of them by the arms, and screamed at him to help her son. The paramedics pleaded with her to let them take Jimmy to the hospital, but she refused to let go of the paramedic's arms—she did not want her son be taken away from her for she feared she would never see him alive again. While the paramedics tried to calm her, Sam's mind began to race. *"I have to get to Jimmy before that ambulance leaves."* Sam opened the back doors to the ambulance and shut them behind him. His father started walking towards the ambulance, but Mrs. Amonte stood in front of him, grabbed both of his arms and said sternly, "Let him be Anthony!"

Mr. Amonte stopped in his tracks. His wife rarely talked to him this way and he knew enough to back off.

Several minutes later, the doors to the ambulance opened and Sam stepped out. He took only three steps before collapsing to the ground. Mrs. Amonte yelled out Sam's name and the paramedics raced to the back of the ambulance to attend to him. As a small crowd gathered, a paramedic got to Sam and began taking his vitals. He tried to assure the Amonte's that Sam was going to be okay and that he had apparently just fainted. He then instructed the other paramedic to go into the ambulance to get some oxygen for Sam. When the paramedic turned to go to the back of the ambulance for the oxygen, he suddenly stopped in his tracks and stood there motionless staring at the back of the ambulance. The other paramedic looked up from Sam and repeated his instructions, "Jack, I need you to get the …" It was at this moment that the he realized the entire crowd had gone quiet and were all looking in the same direction.

At first, it was the movement of the ambulance back door that caught the attention of everyone. Next, it was the lone shoelace that appeared dangling out of the bottom of the door. Soon that shoelace was followed by a baseball cleat, which was followed by a blue sock, which was followed by a pinstriped baseball pant leg. Then, it was all repeated again until there were two pinstriped legs extending out of the back of the ambulance. At that moment, Sam regained consciousness and saw both doors to the ambulance slowly swing open; exposing him to the most beautiful sight he had ever seen—Jimmy sitting on the edge of the ambulance.

Chapter 7

"They're certainly entitled to think that, and they're entitled to full respect for their opinions," said Atticus, "but before I can live with other folks I've got to live with myself. The one thing that doesn't abide by majority rule is a person's conscience."

"What do you think Atticus Finch meant by this?" Mr. Merriman asked his 8th period class. Alexandra raised her hand.

"What are your thoughts Alex?" Mr. Merriman said with a smile.

"Well Mr. M ... This might be a little off topic, but ... one time I was with a group of people at a party, and they were talking about doing umm ... some things that were like ... you know ... *bad*!" Daequan and Paige started to laugh and converse with each other, but Mr. Merriman reminded them to be respectful and not interrupt Alexandra. Alexandra continued, "Well anyways, pretty much everybody was going to do it, not that they are jerks, I mean they are my friends and I knew I could do it too and my parents would have never found out. But I just kept thinking how I would feel later ... I would just feel like cra ... I mean bad."

"Love that analogy Alex," said Mr. Merriman, "and by the way, I am very proud of you for making a good choice."

Daequan looked at her and said, "Oh, you are such an angel, Alex."

Mr. Merriman continued. "So what was it that stopped Atticus *and* Alexandra from doing what everyone else was doing Daequan?"

"I know this—" Daequan responded, "Don't help me ..." Several kids in the room started to laugh. Mr. Merriman put his finger to his mouth and allowed Daequan the time to think. With an uncertain tone, Daequan said, "Their conscience?"

"Exactly Daequan—you nailed it." Mr. Merriman replied.

Alexandra smiled at Daequan and responded with, "Aren't you so special, Daequan?"

Mr. Merriman continued, "There is an old French proverb that I once read that said, 'There is no softer pillow than a clear conscience.' Listen guys, people like Atticus Finch who have the ability to listen to their conscience have been given a great gift. All of you are going to come across situations in your life that will define who you are as a person. Ignoring your conscience can be very tempting. Ignoring your conscience can make life very easy in the short-term; it can make you feel popular, it can get you out of doing things you don't want to do—it could even make you more money. But there is a long-term price to pay for it. At some point, doing what's easy, popular, or just plain wrong is going to catch up with you. One day, when you are all alone thinking about your life, you will realize that you do not like who you are. And this will be a very lonely feeling. However, what this proverb is telling us is when you make moral choices in the course of a day and go to rest your head on your pillow at night, it is going to feel soft as a cloud, and you will sleep like a baby knowing you did the right thing."

From the back of the room, Mason raised his hand tentatively. Mr. Merriman loved it when his most introverted students decided to speak, because he knew that the lesson had special meaning. "Yes Mason?" Mr. Merriman said.

Speaking at a near whisper Mason said, "Mr. Merriman, sometimes I go to bed at night feeling ashamed of myself for what I did, or said during the day. Does that mean that I do not have a conscience?"

Mr. Merriman walked towards the back of the room. All eyes followed him as he sat on an empty desk near Mason and said, "Mason, the fact that you feel that way proves that you *do* have a conscience. Your ability to recognize that you made the wrong choice during the day is a wonderful thing. But here comes the hard part ... your conscience is speaking to you. It's telling you that a change has to be made. Are you going to listen to your conscience? Now, if you listen to your conscience and avoid the choices that may bring you down in the future, then that pillow is going to get softer and softer every night."

Mason raised his hand again and said, "Mr. Merriman do you ever feel like I do?"

Mr. Merriman replied, "Guys do you think my pillow feels soft every single night? Of course not. Like I said on the first day of school, not one of us is perfect, and we all will make mistakes, but the more important question is what are we going to do to correct them? Listen, sometimes when I go to bed my pillow feels like a solid piece of granite. And when it does, I can tell you one thing, I'm going to be walking around the next day with a sledgehammer in my hands. Ask my wife—I love to sleep, and I'm not going two nights in a row without sleep! I'm never going to have a lot of money, and I'm never going to be famous, but I work hard to sleep well at night. I take great pride in that."

"I want to say just one more thing before I show you the movie version of the book. Here is something that you can do every morning to make sure your conscience doesn't become a stranger to you. Look at yourself in the mirror each morning and ask yourself this simple question, 'How did you sleep last night?'"

Mr. Merriman stood there for a moment to let what he said sink in and noticed that every child in the class was looking directly at him. Nothing more needed to be said. No quiz, test, or other assessment had to be given on the topic. They understood.

Mr. Merriman walked to the back of the room, grabbed the television, and wheeled it to the front of the room. He told the class that he was going to show the 1962 movie version of *To Kill a Mockingbird* starring Gregory Peck. Before he got the chance to say anything about the movie, many of the kids started asking him who was going to be able to sit in the old leather rocker recliner he had in the back of the class during the movie. He always chose one deserving student to sit in the chair during a movie. However, if a student asked if he or she could sit in the chair, he would never let them.

Daequan thought that he would outsmart Mr. Merriman and said, "Mr. M, you should sit in the chair today. You've been on your feet all day."

Mr. Merriman replied, "Once again Daequan, you're the voice of reason. I think that's a great idea!" The entire class moaned, and Mr. Merriman smiled ear to ear.

"Now back to the movie guys. First of all, this movie is a classic, and yes, it is in black and white." The entire class moaned once again. Mr. Merriman smiled and said, "Believe me, you're going to get angry every time the bell rings at the end of the period because you're going to want to see more."

Mr. Merriman started the DVD and then shut off the lights. When the movie started, he walked to the back of the room and sat in the recliner to grade papers.

Mr. Merriman was correct, the kids loved the movie, and when the bell rang signaling the period, they all groaned. Instead of getting up immediately to dismiss the class, Mr. Merriman kept the lights off and let the movie run past the bell. At first, the students thought that he just wanted them to finish viewing this key scene in the movie before they left, but after several minutes, the kids started looking back at Mr. Merriman to see if he was going to turn on the lights and dismiss them. Daequan started laughing because he thought Mr. Merriman was pretending to be asleep. Olivia, who was sitting in the back of the room closest to him, was the first to sense that something was wrong. She called out to Mr. Merriman, but he did not respond. However, Olivia knew something was wrong and yelled for someone to turn on the lights.

Olivia rose from her seat and knelt down in front of Mr. Merriman and said, "Mr. M? Mr. Merriman? Are you okay?"

When he didn't respond, Olivia reached up and gently shook his shoulders. When his head fell backwards, lifeless, on to the headrest of the chair, Olivia screamed in horror.

Mr. Merriman's life ended at age 41 with a sudden stroke in the middle of his 8th period class.

Chapter 8

"There he is. He's coming down the hall—ask him."
No—you ask him!"

"Daniel, you ask him, he lives on your street. Here he comes—ask him!"

The two students waited until Sam was a few feet away and blurted out the question that everyone in town wanted to know, "Hey Amonte—did you bring Jimmy back from the dead?"

All the students nearby turned to Sam to listen to his answer, but Sam just kept walking down the hall to homeroom. He was not prepared for what he was experiencing at school this day. He noticed that as soon as his mother dropped him off at school, all the students and teachers were staring at him and whispering to each other as he walked into school and down the hallways.

Just before he reached his homeroom, Sam heard someone yell out from down the hallway, "Hey Amonte—my dog died last week; if I dig him up and bring him to your house tonight, can you give him mouth to mouth?"

Sam walked to his seat in the front of the class and sat down. Homeroom was one of the noisiest classes of the day, but this morning you could hear a pin drop. Sam could feel all eyes in the room watching his every move. Even Sam's homeroom teacher Mr. Foglia was acting weird. Mr. Foglia always said good morning to Sam and asked him how his weekend was on Monday morning. However, on this particular Monday, Mr. Foglia did not utter one word to him. The silence was too much for Sam to take, so he turned around, and shot a look of anger at the rest of the class and yelled, "Stop staring at me!"

Mr. Foglia intervened, "Sam, please calm down, and the rest of you, stop staring at him." Some of the kids looked away and started talking, but others could not take their eyes off Sam.

After what seemed like an hour, but was only five minutes, the bell for first period rang and Sam was the first one out the door. Sam tried to get to his next class before the hallways became crowded again, but the events at the baseball field caused students to congregate in small groups throughout the hallways so they could get a glimpse of Sam. When he saw a large group of kids at the end of the hall, he decided to duck into the bathroom.

Sam's plan was to stay in the bathroom until the halls cleared out. As he sat in the stall with the door closed, he heard several boys enter the bathroom.

"Yeah, I was at the game." one of the boys said.

"Did you see him come out of the ambulance?" the other boy asked.

"No, I didn't actually see him come out of the ambulance, but I talked to Pam and she said her little sister saw him go into the ambulance and then walk out a few minutes later."

"So you didn't actually see Amonte do anything?"

"No—but I will tell you something, I saw Jimmy get hit with the ball, and I saw the ambulance drivers wheel him off the field. He was dead!"

Another boy entered the conversation.

"I don't know who to believe, and people are saying all different kinds of things happened. Some people said they saw him go into the ambulance. Some said they only saw him coming out. Others said that they didn't see him go in or come out. Some other people were even saying that they saw an old man inside of the ambulance with him. I don't know what's true or who to believe, but I will tell you what; I am staying away from that Amonte kid. Either way, he is either a liar or just a plain freak!"

As soon as the boy finished his sentence, Sam came bursting out of the stall. He ran so fast and out of control that he knocked one kid on to the floor and another into the bathroom mirror shattering it. Running from the bathroom, Sam ran directly into the assistant principal who grabbed him by the arm. Sam yanked his arm away, and ran out the front doors of the school.

About a half hour later, Sam arrived home to find his mother waiting on the porch for him. The school had already called Mrs. Amonte to let her know that he had left school. She was standing at the top of the stairs with her apron on and a dishtowel thrown over her shoulder. As Sam walked up the stairs of the porch, he threw his arms around her, and his mother grabbed her dishtowel and wiped the tears and sweat from his eyes.

After a few minutes, he gained his composure and his mother said, "Sam, let's sit down on the porch and talk." He sat in the old steel chair while Mrs. Amonte knelt before him. "What happened today at school, honey?"

"Mom, as soon as you dropped me off, all the kids were staring at me and talking about me because of what happened with Jimmy. Some kids in the bathroom called me a 'liar' and a 'freak'."

"Honey, I can't explain what happened with Jimmy. I don't know if anyone will ever be able to explain what happened. But I know one thing; you are *not* a liar, and you are *not* a freak."

Sam looked down at his mother and said, "Mom, do you believe that I saved Jimmy's life?"

"Sam, from the moment you were born, I knew that you were going to be special. When they laid you into my arms for the first time and I saw your beautiful little face, I just knew it. Your grandmother said the same thing when she first held you. I believe that God has endowed all of us with gifts to share with one another. The empathy and sympathy that you show towards all living things is your gift to share. You should not turn your back on it; you should embrace that gift."

"But Mom—do you believe that I saved Jimmy's life?"

"Sweetie, my mind tells me that it is impossible—"

"So *you* don't even believe me?"

41

"Hold on—let me finish. If I read a story in the paper about what happened at the ball field, I would find it hard to believe that a person would have the ability to bring another back to life. That is my mind talking to me. However … my heart tells me something very different. No one knows you better than I do. I have seen the signs over the years. I have seen the way you interact with others. Your ability to connect with and understand people and animals is amazing and deeply moving to me. I've seen people I have known for years and total strangers connect with you in so many meaningful ways. They meet you and your compassion and understanding seem to transform them. It's as though their burdens of life are lifted. I see it in their eyes and in their body language. Their shoulders straighten, their chins rise, their eyes brighten—there is a sense of renewal and hope when you connect with them."

She placed both her hands on Sam's cheeks to make sure that Sam focused on her words.

"So if you tell me that *you* saved Jimmy, I believe you."

Chapter 9

The weather was crisp and cold the day of the funeral mass for Mr. Merriman. Tiny whirlwinds of dust-like snow slithered across the road and sparkled in the mid-morning sun. The Church of St. Andrew's was packed with mourners—as many as seven hundred people were in attendance. So many showed up on this day, that the church staff had to set up a tent with heaters and loudspeakers on the steps of the church to accommodate the throngs who came to participate in the ceremony. From the loudspeakers they could hear Father Paulson reading from the Book of Wisdom, "*But the souls of the just are in the hand of God, and no torment shall touch them. They seemed, in the view of the foolish, to be dead; and their passing away was thought an affliction and their going forth from us, utter destruction. But they are in peace ...*"

In the front row of the church were Mr. Merriman's wife and his three daughters. Their faces showed a mixture of expressions—both shock and grief. All this had happened too suddenly for them to handle. In the next section of the church were Mr. Merriman's relatives who had apparently come from all across the country. His three brothers, two sisters, grandparents, aunts, uncles, nieces, nephews, and cousins came from places as far away as England, Australia, Seattle and California. Behind his relatives were his closest friends. Even though Mr. Merriman had an enormous family, the number of people considered to be close friends was ten times the number of relatives that attended the mass that day. However, the single largest group of mourners present that day were the people who had crossed paths with Mr. Merriman during his years as a teacher. From the second half of the church and sprawled out onto the steps and into the parking lot were the hundreds of students who had come to pay their last respects to the man who touched their lives so positively. Mr. Merriman was truly blessed.

Father Paulson was now reading from the Gospel of John, Chapter 5, *"One man was there who had been ill for thirty-eight years. When Jesus saw him lying there and knew that he had been ill for a long time, he said to him, "Do you want to be well?" The sick man answered him, "Sir, I have no one to put me into the pool when the water is stirred up; while I am on my way, someone else gets down there before me. Jesus said to him, "Rise, take up your mat, and walk. Immediately the man became well, took up his mat, and walked."*

Olivia, Daequan, Alexandra, Alex, Paige, Clare, Mason, and Andrew were all listening to Father Paulson's words as they sat together in the last pew in the church with the rest of Mr. Merriman's 8th period class.   All of them were finding it very difficult to focus on the readings. They wanted so much to be able to celebrate Mr. Merriman's wonderful life, but all they could picture in their minds was Mr. Merriman slumped in the chair.

Father Paulson continued, *"They asked him, "Who is the man who told you, 'Take it up and walk'?...Jesus answered and said to them, "Amen, amen, I say to you, a son cannot do anything on his own, but only what he sees his father doing; for what he does, his son will do also. For the Father loves his Son and shows him everything that he himself does, and he will show him greater works than these, so that you may be amazed. For just as the Father raises the dead and gives life, so also does the Son give life to whomever he wishes..."*

After the serving of communion, Father Paulson came to the pulpit and announced that two students of Mr. Merriman would be saying a few words. As Father Paulson stepped away from the pulpit, the sound of people getting up in the back echoed throughout the church. The crowd of mourners all seemed to turn their heads in unison to see who was getting up to speak for Mr. Merriman. Those in the aisle seats could see a beautiful young red-haired girl dressed in a black skirt and white silken top making her way from the pew to the aisle. Upon making it to the aisle, she paused a second, and waited for a young man in a wheelchair dressed in a blue suit and shiny patent leather shoes to pull up beside her. As they made their way down the aisle to the front of the church, the sounds of the motor from the boy's wheelchair and girl's high-heeled shoes echoed throughout the church.

Just before getting to the altar, the young boy and girl made their way over to Mrs. Merriman and her daughters and gave each of them a white rose. All eyes were focused on these two teenagers, as pallbearers lifted the boy's wheelchair up onto the altar. They then made their way to the pulpit.

The young girl spoke first, "Good Morning, my name is Olivia Pinchot." She then passed the microphone to the young boy. He sat up very straight in his wheelchair and said, "And my name is Andrew Lambert. We would like to say a few words about Mr. Merriman. Mr. Merriman, forgive us if our grammar is not exactly perfect." For the first time during the service, Mrs. Merriman smiled.

Olivia was the first to speak. As she took her place at the pulpit, rays of sunshine began streaking across the altar. The sunshine showed so brightly across the altar that it caused Olivia to squint and shield her eyes. As Olivia struggled to read the piece of paper that she brought up to the altar, she suddenly stopped.

She stood in front of these hundreds of mourners, took a deep breath, closed her eyes, and bathed herself in the warmth of the sunlight. After about a minute, a wonderful smile came across her face that was so bright and beautiful that the sun itself should have felt insecure. When Olivia opened her eyes, she folded up the piece of paper and put it in the front pocket of her blouse.

"This is the way it felt to be a student in Mr. Merriman's class …" Olivia closed her eyes again and felt the warmth of the sun upon her face.

"Mr. Merriman was our sun. He was the center of our universe, and all of us could not help but feel the intense gravitational pull of his personality. When I first sat in his class, his wit, wisdom, and personality shined so brightly upon me that I had to shield my eyes the first few days. I had never experienced a teacher who cared so much about my mind and soul. It was almost too much for me to handle. But like all of us, my eyes *and* my heart began to adjust to the warmth and brightness of Mr. M. From that point on, I looked forward to coming to his class every day and basking in the glow of the most wonderful person I have ever met."

Olivia paused for a moment and wiped tears from her eyes and ended with, "From this point on in my life, every cloudy day will be a sorrowful reminder that he is gone. However ... every time I feel the warmth of the sun upon my face, I will fondly remember the gifts Mr. M gave to me each day. Gifts that will last a lifetime."

Olivia looked down at Andrew, hugged him, and then passed the microphone to him. Andrew went to speak, but at first, nothing came out. Andrew adjusted himself in his chair, straightened his back and tried to continue. When he did, his voice was strong and forceful.

"For most of my life, I have faced nothing but pain and disappointment. When I was younger, I would wake up each morning, look down at my legs lying on the bed, and hope to see just one little movement from under the blankets. But day after day, week after week, month after month and year after year, nothing ever happened. Then one morning I just ... gave up. As a matter of fact, I gave up on not only myself, but the entire world. What was I going to contribute to society when I couldn't even perform the simplest tasks without help? When I came to this realization, it was like I built a concrete wall between myself and the rest of the world. It was like being in solitary confinement with the person I hated the most."

"Then I came into Mr. Merriman's class. I'll be honest … the first few weeks in his class were brutal for me. I couldn't stand Mr. M. Every single day it was like he was trying to break into my fortified world."

Andrew continued with his best Mr. Merriman imitation, *"Hey Lambert-did your girlfriend write this paper for you again? Lambert—what did you do this weekend? Tell us about it? Stop staring at the girls walking by Lambert! Lambert, I can't help it, you know you're my favorite student."*

People began laughing.

Andrew continued, "When he talked to me, sometimes I would answer in a simple phrase, but most of the time I didn't answer him at all. If I were Mr. Merriman, I would have given up on me long ago. But I am not Mr. Merriman; in fact, no one is like Mr. Merriman."

"Every day when I came into class, it was like he could instantly read my feelings and knew exactly what I needed to hear on that day. Sometimes it came via a joke, sometimes in a conversation after class, or sometimes as part of a lesson." Then Andrew stopped speaking to the crowd and started speaking towards Mr. Merriman's coffin in a quiet conversational tone. "Mr. M, how did you know?" Andrew paused and became choked up with emotion. "How did you know that when I went to bed at night I hated who I was? How did you know that I was suffocating behind that concrete wall?"

Andrew began to speak to the audience once again. "Mr. Merriman chipped at that wall every single day, slowly and surely. At first, *he* did all the hard labor. But as the school year went on, he taught me how to chip away at it myself. And he loved it best when *I* did the work; every time I answered a question, volunteered to read, helped another classmate or even cracked a joke, he would just give me that look that said, 'Keep up the good work Lambert!'. Like Mr. Merriman did, I love my life now. And when I go to bed at night, for the first time in a very long time, I love myself. Mr. Merriman taught me that strength of character and generosity of the heart was more important than the strength of my legs."

Andrew looked back to Mr. Merriman's casket again and said, "Mr. Merriman ... I want you to know that this apprentice and *all* of your apprentices who are assembled here today are ready to carry on the work of our master teacher."

Just as Andrew finished those words, all 130 of Mr. Merriman's students started walking in a line towards the front of the church. Each student was wearing a white t-shirt with a large gold colored sledgehammer on the front. Centered on the back, was a smaller graphic depicting two hands holding a hammer and chisel. Below this were the words, *"How did you sleep last night?"*

As each student came before the casket, they bowed, and then moved along to Mrs. Merriman in the front pew. As they stood before Mrs. Merriman, each one expressed his or her condolences and handed her a sealed envelope. Daequan had come up with the idea that each student should complete one more assignment for Mr. Merriman. The assignment was to write either a poem or short narrative honoring his memory.

As the last student handed her envelope to Mrs. Merriman, Andrew concluded his comments. "As painful as this is for all of us here to face the future without you Mr. M, there is great comfort knowing that God has no doubt provided you with the softest pillow there is in heaven."

Chapter 10

Sam felt a great sense of relief upon hearing that his mother believed in him; however that feeling was short lived. As Sam and Mrs. Amonte sat on the porch, Mr. Amonte came screeching into the driveway looking very agitated. Mr. Amonte brought the car to an abrupt stop, opened the car door, and was holding up a newspaper.

"Did you see this?" he yelled. "Look at this! I knew this was going to happen!" Sam and Mrs. Amonte looked at him puzzled.

Mr. Amonte continued, "Look at this article—" Mr. Amonte threw the newspaper into Sam's lap. Sam and his mother looked down at the newspaper and the headline read, "*Miracle at the Ballpark*".

"Do you realize the problems this is going to create?" Mr. Amonte snarled.

Mrs. Amonte said to him, "Calm down Anthony—let me read the article." Mrs. Amonte began reading aloud the article that appeared in Monday's edition of the *Times Union*.

"*Miracle at the Ballpark. In the space of just one hour, the lives of one Rochester, New York family went from utter tragedy to triumphant jubilation. On Saturday, June 1st, a local boy was struck violently in the chest by a baseball during a championship baseball game and pronounced dead at the scene by paramedics. An event such as this usually ends in utter tragedy—a young, promising teenager gone much too soon and a family left to wonder why it had to happen to their loving, innocent son. Only this story does not end here ...*"

Mrs. Amonte continued reading the article—alternating between reading it aloud and to herself. "*...Witnesses at the scene then reported that a 17 year-old teenager, Samuel Amonte* *entered the ambulance ... some time later, the boy was sitting on the edge of the ambulance alive."*

"Nine year-old, Sarah Brozniak said, 'I saw Sam go into the ambulance after they put Jimmy's body in the back. Then about 3-4 minutes later, Sam came out and passed out. Then just a few minutes after that—Jimmy was alive.'"

"James Flanigan, 33, who was at the scene, maintained that at no point did he see the teenager Amonte enter or exit the ambulance. Flanigan said, 'I was standing near the ambulance the entire time. I saw them put the poor kid's body in the ambulance. People around here are losing their minds; to say that a 17 year-old boy brought another kid back to life is ridiculous. This is an affront to the Lord Our Savior. This boy will answer to the Lord some day. No miracle occurred here. The paramedics obviously screwed up on this one. '"

"Pastor Michael Jemison of St. Marks's Lutheran Church disagreed, 'I believe that this boy (Amonte), with the help of the Lord, saved Jimmy's life. This boy has a special relationship with the Lord our Savior.'"

Mr. Amonte interrupted Mrs. Amonte, "Do you see that? This is only the beginning! They aren't going to leave us alone. We are not going to be able to live in peace. People think he is some messenger from God or something. Guys at work, guys I see every single day, eat lunch with, bowl with couldn't even look me in the eye today. They think we're some kind of freaks. This one woman I work with walked into the break room when I was alone and asked if Sam could come over her house and meet her sickly mother and *'lay his hands on her'*. What the hell is that?"

"Anthony just calm down—you are making Sam out to be the bad guy here. He did nothing wrong!" she yelled.

"I told him to stay away and leave Jimmy alone. He had to go into the ambulance ..."

"But he saved Jimmy's life, Anthony!" Mrs. Amonte shouted.

Mr. Amonte slumped back when he heard these words from his wife. He looked at her incredulously and said, "Jenny, are you telling me that *you* believe that Sam brought Jimmy back to life?"

"Yes, I do, Anthony."

Mr. Amonte stared at his wife with a mixture of shock and disbelief. He could think of nothing to say to her; he stormed past her, slammed the screen door to the front porch, and stomped up the stairs to the second floor. Mrs. Amonte ran up the stairs after her husband. Sam sat on the porch the entire time picturing the pain and anguish on his mother's face during the confrontation with his father. Horrible waves of guilt passed over him as he listened to his parents arguing into the evening.

When Sam woke up the next morning, he hoped that things would be better between his mother and father. Once he was ready for school, Sam came down to the breakfast table only to find his parents sitting there in silence. His mother asked Sam if he wanted some scrambled eggs and toast, but Sam said that he was not hungry. Soon after his father rose from the table, picked up his briefcase, and walked right past his mother without saying goodbye or kissing her. For as long as he could remember, Sam's parents always kissed each other goodbye as his father went off to work. Mrs. Amonte stood there standing in the middle of the kitchen for several moments in the hope that she would hear the side door open again and find her husband coming back to embrace her. But he did not return.

She walked past Sam, kissed him on the cheek, told him to get to school, then walked upstairs. As he walked out of the house, he could hear his mother quietly sobbing in her bedroom.

Sam's second day at school after the incident was simply a repeat of the first. This continued for the rest of the week, and soon the second and third weeks were just another repeat of the first. Sam hoped that people would grow tired and disinterested as time went on, but instead of dissipating, interest in the event just intensified. The situation was becoming unbearable for Sam.

There was no escape from the situation; he had to face it for seven and a half hours at school, then for the rest of the day at home. His parents barely spoke to each other for weeks. He had no idea that things were about to get even worse.

Several days before graduation, Sam was walking home from school, and just as he turned the corner onto his street, he spotted several vehicles in front of his house. Sam became concerned at the sight of the vehicles, and this caused him to pick up his pace. Upon getting closer, Sam realized that these vehicles were owned by two local television stations—Channels 10 and 13. When he arrived at his house, two cameramen and two reporters were on his porch talking to his mother through the screen door. As he stepped onto the porch stairs, he heard one of the reporters say,

"Mrs. Amonte, just give us a few minutes of your time. We just want to talk to you and your son. People want to know what happened on that day. I promise—"

Just then the television crews realized that Sam was on the porch. Immediately the crews and reporters surrounded Sam and started firing off questions, "Sam did you bring your friend Jimmy back to life?"

"Sam, people feel that you are a messenger of God; have you ever spoken to or seen God?

"Why don't you help more people with your gift?"

"Some people think that you are using this accident as a way to gain attention. Has your family made any money off this?"

Mrs. Amonte rushed out the screen door and began pushing away the reporters and yelling at the reporters, "Leave my son alone!" The Channel 10 reporter told Mrs. Amonte not to touch him and grabbed Mrs. Amonte's arm. Just then, Mr. Amonte pulled into the driveway and stormed out of the car. The sight of the vans, reporters, and cameras had him enraged. When he saw the reporter with his hands on his wife, it sent him over the edge. Mr. Amonte came charging into the cameramen and reporters, first knocking the Channel 13 cameraman to the ground. When the Channel 13 reporter saw him coming, he quickly and wisely stepped aside. The Channel 10 reporter who had grabbed Mrs. Amonte was not so lucky—Mr. Amonte threw a punch that caught him totally off guard. The force of the blow sent the reporter sprawling across the front lawn. The Channel 10 cameraman caught the entire incident on film, which was replayed repeatedly over the next few days.

Within minutes, a police car arrived on the scene, and the last thing Sam saw was his father being handcuffed and placed in a squad car. Although his mother characterized what happened with Jimmy as a gift, Sam could not see it. This so-called gift had turned out to be a curse, and Sam knew that something had to be done about it before it destroyed his family.

Chapter 11

Around 1 a.m. the morning of Sam's high school graduation, Sam lay on his bed wide awake. He was fully clothed and had on his high-topped green *Converse* sneakers. Beside his bed was a duffle bag and jacket.

At approximately 1:15, Sam put on his jacket, grabbed a pillowcase, slung his duffle bag over his shoulder, opened the door to his bedroom and quietly made his way down the stairs to the foyer. With his pillowcase in hand, he walked through the kitchen and made his way down to the basement food pantry to fill up on some supplies. With each careful step, Sam shuddered at the long, groaning creak that signaled his descent down the basement stairs.

When he was done filling the pillowcase, Sam made his way back up the stairs.

As he was walking through the kitchen to go out the back door, he noticed a dark figure sitting at the head of the kitchen table. The sight of the figure in the darkness stopped Sam dead in his tracks. As his eyes strained to make out the figure at the table, Sam finally realized who it was—it was his father sitting in the chair with his hands folded on the table.

A million thoughts raced through Sam's head while he stood there trying to figure out what to say. But Sam suddenly realized something; his father did not say a word to him either. No, *"What are you doing?"* or *"Where are you going?"* Nothing. Then it suddenly dawned on Sam why his father was silent. His father *wanted* him to leave.

With this wrenching realization, he swung his duffle bag over his back, opened the back door and quietly slipped away into the night.

After preparing breakfast, Mrs. Amonte entered Sam's room to wake him up for the graduation ceremony and immediately noticed that something was wrong. Sam's bed did not look like it had been slept in the previous night, and several things seemed to be missing from his room. She immediately rushed through the house calling for him, but he did not respond. With each unanswered call she became more frantic. After going through the entire house, she raced back up the stairs again to Sam's room hoping he would crawl out from under his bed laughing at the joke he just played on her. However, she knew he was gone. Sam's most prized possessions were missing: the picture with Jimmy at summer camp, the signed baseball by Cal Ripken, and the varsity letter he earned as a freshman for baseball. Feeling faint, she sat down on the edge of Sam's bed with her face cupped in her hands. When she lifted her head from her hands, she spotted an envelope on the nightstand. The envelope was addressed to "Mom". It read:

Dear Mom,

I know that you must be feeling confused, upset and hurt right now. Ma, you know that the last thing that I would ever want to do is hurt you. You have always been the one person in my life that has always been there for me. You made it clear to me each day, that no matter what I did or failed to do, that you would always love me. From my oldest memory of you picking me up and cradling me in your arms in the kitchen, to our talks on the front porch, you always gave your love unconditionally. You will never know just how much this has meant to me over my life and how much it has helped me get through the tough times. It is a feeling that I will carry with me forever. I know that I have no right to ask anything else of you, but I really need you to understand why I am leaving.

I know this may be hard for you to understand, but I am leaving because I love you and Dad. You and Dad love each other very much and have always had a good marriage. You two have created a wonderful life for yourselves. However, lately, you and Dad have been arguing a lot. I can't ever recall you two arguing so often. Let's be honest—it is all because of me. The last thing that I would ever want to do is jeopardize what you have with Dad. However, that is exactly what I am doing.

I don't know why I have been given this power. It took me years to recognize that I had it, let alone figure out what it is. At first, I thought this power was a good thing, but as time has gone by, I've realized that it comes with a price. I don't regret helping Jimmy at all. The only thing I regret is the impact it has had on our family—particularly Dad. I just don't understand why from the very beginning he thought this was such a terrible thing. I never intentionally wanted to hurt anything or anyone. Something just comes over me when I see something in pain. It just seems so unnatural to sit by and watch someone or something in pain. Yet, for the past several years, I have had to fight this innate urge. I fought it because I love Dad and wanted to make him happy and proud, but I clearly haven't been able to do that. If I follow my instincts and be myself, it causes problems for you and Dad. If I live my life being someone who I am not, I am unhappy. At this point, I do not know what to do, but I am not going to stand by and watch your marriage fall apart while I try to figure this whole thing out.

Ma, remember I am eighteen years old. I am a mature, strong, and intelligent man who can take care of himself. Remember, Dad left home when he was younger than I was, and he did very well for himself. I may not be the person Dad wants me to be, but I feel I have a pretty good head on my shoulders and could achieve anything I set out to do. So please don't worry, I am going to be fine. I promise that I will contact you from time to time to let you know that I am okay.

I love you with all my heart Ma. Tell Dad that I love him too. I will miss you both.

Sam

P.S. Please tell Jimmy good-bye and I will miss him.

Chapter 12

Mr. Massina, Principal of Cayuga High School, leaned back in this leather chair, pinched the bridge of his nose and gave a heavy sigh wondering if he could get through just one more interview. In front of him were ten file folders containing personnel information on the applicants to replace Mr. Merriman. Mr. Massina had gone through nine interviews since 9:00 that morning and was no closer to finding a replacement. He hoped that this last interview would prove to be more fruitful than the others.

While Mr. Massina would never describe Mr. Merriman as a close friend, he respected him immensely. Mr. Merriman was everything he wanted in his teachers—hardworking, intelligent, and reliable. He could never recall a single negative comment from a student about Mr. Merriman, and while it is virtually impossible for any teacher to escape the critical judgment of parents, he could only recall one instance where he received a parental complaint regarding him. Mr. Massina knew he was not going to find the caliber of teacher that Mr. Merriman was, so he simply resigned himself to finding an applicant who would provide structure and discipline to the students whose lives had been turned upside down by Mr. Merriman's death.

In the main office, adjacent to Mr. Massina's, sat the last applicant of the day. The applicant, roughly late thirties in age, was dressed impeccably in a dark blue, pinstriped, Brooks Brothers suit; white shirt with French cuffs, and a yellow paisley tie. He was clean-shaven with short, dark brown hair and green eyes flecked with gold.

When the last applicant first arrived and introduced himself to the secretarial staff, he found the staff to be cordial and professional. However, as he turned his back to them to sit down, the two secretaries looked at each other with raised eyebrows and mouthed the word, *"Wow!"* As soon as he sat down and faced them again, the secretaries quickly put on their best professional faces and acted as if they were engrossed in their daily routines.

Mr. Massina's executive secretary, Mrs. Gillette, said to the applicant, "Mr. Massina will be with you in a few moments."

He responded politely with a smile, "Thank you very much, Mrs. Gillette."

Mrs. Gillette smiled back and was impressed that he had already memorized her name. After five minutes passed, Mrs. Gillette said, "Mr. Massina will see you now. You may go in."

As the applicant entered the office, Mr. Massina walked out from behind his desk, extended his hand and said, "Pleased to meet you."

"Nice to meet you as well, Mr. Massina. Thank you for the opportunity."

"Please have a seat and let's talk," said Mr. Massina.

Mr. Massina opened up the interview by informing the applicant about the various steps of the interview process. Next, he moved into the questioning phase of the interview by asking him a series of questions: his strengths and weaknesses as a teacher, describing a typical lesson in his class, classroom management philosophy, "what if" scenarios—all the standard educational interview questions. Mr. Massina acted as though he was pleased with the applicant's responses.

Towards the end of the interview, Mr. Massina closed the interview folder, looked the applicant intently in the eyes and said, "I am impressed with many of your responses today, and I think that you could be a good fit here at Cayuga, but there is one thing about your past experiences that concerns me that I would like you to expand upon."

Mr. Massina opened the file once again, glanced at his resume and said, "While you have had many varied and rich educational experiences, it seems as though you have not stayed very long in one place. I see here that you have taught in Las Vegas, Los Angeles, El Paso, Minneapolis, Detroit, and Cleveland. I love the fact that you have taught such a diverse group of students, subjects, and levels, but why is it that you have moved so much over your career?"

The applicant looked down for a second, and then responded, "Mr. Massina, I worked many jobs before going into education, and somehow I saved enough to put myself through college. I have worked very hard to get where I am today. At first, I loved moving from place to place; it was exciting to experience the different places and people along the way. However, as I have become older, I have found myself longing for a place that I could call home. If you give me the opportunity to teach here at Cayuga, I would like this to be the last entry on my resume. I have been living in the community for about three months now and would love to make this my home."

Mr. Massina smiled and said, "I appreciate your honesty and candor. I think that you would be a good fit here at Cayuga. When you leave the office I am going to make a call to our personnel director recommending your employment."

"Thank you *so* much for the opportunity, Mr. Massina."

"You are welcome. By the way, there is one more thing I would like to tell you. This is a rather unique and sensitive teaching situation that you have applied for. The position you are applying for is vacant because the previous English teacher recently passed away. What made the situation even more tragic was the fact that he died in school right in front of his eighth period class. Needless to say, the students he taught are still reeling from this. He was one of our most revered teachers; it might prove to be a challenge for you teaching in his shadow. Do you think you will be able to handle this?"

"I will make sure that I return structure and calm to their classes, Mr. Massina. I will be able to handle it," he responded.

Mr. Massina, shook the applicant's hand, led him out to the main hallway, and once again mentioned that the district's personnel director would be calling him within the next few days. As the two men parted, the applicant turned and walked down the main corridor, all the while looking at the various awards, plaques and pictures hanging on the walls. Just as he came to the main doors, he noticed a large framed picture with a plaque. The man in the picture seemed familiar to him, yet he could not place him. When he stepped closer to the plaque to read the inscription, it read as follows, *In Memory of James K. Merriman 1968-2009.*

When the applicant read the name on the plaque, his heart dropped. The man in the photograph, the teacher who recently died, the person who he was about to replace was the boy whose life he had saved nearly twenty-four years ago on the baseball field—his best friend Jimmy.

Chapter 13

The night before he was about to take over Jimmy's job, Sam had deep reservations. Several times during the last two days, he had fought off the urge to contact Principal Massina and call the whole thing off. Sam had spent twenty-four years trying to put the past to rest, and just when he was about to start a new beginning in a place he had finally chose to call home, the past jumped out once again to try and snatch it away from him.

While Sam's response to Massina about why he moved so frequently was partially true, Sam was not completely honest in the interview. When Sam left home at age 18, he worked for several years at various jobs to save enough to put himself through school. However, once he gained employment as a teacher, he wasn't necessarily moving from place to place to "see the country". He always left for the same reason.

Each one of Sam's positions as a teacher would inevitably follow the same set of circumstances. Sam would start off the first several years with excellent appraisals from his administrators. He would also be known for establishing outstanding relationships with staff members, parents, and students in the district where he was employed. All signs would point to Sam settling down in the area, establishing tenure, and enjoying a successful career. However, that path was never realized. His stops in Las Vegas, Los Angeles, El Paso, Minneapolis, Detroit, and Cleveland all ended the same way— Sam having to leave before trouble started.

Invariably, in each teaching situation, Sam would come across people who needed his gift. Despite the fact that his gift wreaked havoc on his early life and family, Sam continually tried to fight off his strong feelings of compassion and empathy. In most of the situations, Sam simply left his position because he could no longer stand to be a witness to the suffering of an individual. He knew that if he stayed, his natural instincts would take over, and he would find himself dealing with the same level of attention that Jimmy's healing brought on. However, on two occasions Sam's innate instinct got the best of him, and he performed his gift of healing.

On one occasion, Sam purposefully waited to perform his gift on the last day of school, so that he could quickly tender his resignation and leave town before trouble started. On another occasion, Sam was so overtaken with compassion that he performed his gift in the middle of the school year. In that situation, Sam simply informed the district that he had a serious illness in his family and had to resign his position and leave town to care for a family member.

On those same occasions, Sam learned of yet another negative aspect to his gift; the physical toll that it wreaked upon his body. As he grew older, he suffered physical effects from the performance of his gift.

At age 40, Sam was emotionally and physically exhausted. He simply wanted to live a normal life. He wanted a place to call home. He wanted to settle down in one place. He wanted normalcy in his life. However, he realized that this was never going to happen if he did not change who he was as a person. Those intense qualities of compassion, empathy, and sympathy were going to have to be suppressed. In this new position, he was going to have to detach himself emotionally from the people he met. He convinced himself that he didn't have to become emotionally involved with his students to be an effective teacher. His exceptional intellect, knowledge of his subject area, and great lesson planning were all he needed to be successful. He was through performing his gift.

Cayuga was the start of a new beginning, and he was determined to make this his last stop.

Chapter 14

"What did he say to you when you told him that you were worried about Paige?" Alexandra asked Daequan at the lunch table.

"Mr. Amonte just told me to go the Guidance Office and see one of the school counselors about it," answered Daequan.

"So he didn't even ask you what was going on with her or why you were worried about her?"

"Nope. Nothing. He just walked out of his room and said that he had to go to a meeting."

Alexandra continued, "I don't get him … Mr. Amonte's really smart, and I am learning in his class, but it just seems like he only cares about English. He's nothing like—"

"Wait—don't even go there," Andrew interrupted. "Listen, no one is going to be like Mr. Merriman. Look at the rest of the teachers in the school; none of them are like Mr. M. Did you really think his sub would be like him? If Mr. M were here, he would tell us not to judge him so quickly. He always told us not to compare ourselves with other people. Just do the best you can and try to become a better person. Maybe Mr. Amonte is doing the best he can right now."

Alexandra answered, "I know, but this guy seems like he doesn't even like being with us. The only time I see any emotion in him is when he talks about a novel we are reading."

While Daequan, Alexandra, and Andrew were having their conversation in the lunchroom, Mr. Massina and Sam were meeting in his office to discuss his performance over the last two months.

Mr. Massina started the meeting with the following. "Sam, how do you feel you have performed here over the past few months?"

"Mr. Massina, I have been working extremely hard. I spend all my planning time during the school day working on lessons and go home after school and work on them until about midnight each night. I think I have developed some excellent units for my students. I have developed some great lessons for our upcoming unit on *Night* by Elie Wiesel."

"And how are your students doing, Sam?"

"I am pleased with their performance so far. Since arriving, I have noticed steady improvement in test scores and in the writing pieces they are handing in. Their behavior so far has been excellent. I think providing them with clear and consistent expectations have helped them."

"Sam," Mr. Massina said, "when I asked you how the students were doing, I meant, how they are doing emotionally, particularly with the death of Mr. Merriman?"

Sam sat there for a moment and was at a loss for words. Sam had spent so much time and energy preparing lessons and trying to put Jimmy and his past out of his mind that he realized he could not even answer the question. He had no idea how they were doing emotionally. He hadn't even mentioned Mr. Merriman's name in class nor had an informal conversation between classes with any student about him.

Mr. Massina knew that Sam did not have an answer to his question and broke the awkward silence in the room.

"Sam, you have a tremendous amount of potential. I have been in your classroom to observe you over eight times since you arrived. Your lesson planning is top notch, and your command of the subject area is quite impressive. I know that your students are learning; I see that happening in your classroom. But I have to be honest with you; this is Cayuga High and people would kill to have a shot at working here. I have many potential candidates who are great at lesson planning and are highly knowledgeable in their subject matter, but I want someone who can bring more than that to the students in my school. I have talked to some of your colleagues, the guidance counselors, and many of the kids.

All of them basically say the same thing about you—your lessons are excellent and you're smart. But after that, they have nothing more to say. They all just stop after mentioning those two attributes, and I sense that they have more to say, but they don't want to say it because it is negative. So I push them a little bit more. Now don't be upset, remember it is my job to know how my teachers are performing, but they all feel that your connections with kids are weak."

"I have been a principal for over 25 years and I am very upfront with new teachers. I tell them exactly what areas they need to improve in, and I give them the advice and resources to get them to where I need them to be. If they don't act upon that advice or utilize those resources, then they do not return the following year."

Sam asked Mr. Massina, "Are you telling me that I am not going to be returning to Cayuga this September?"

Mr. Massina replied, "I have not made that decision yet, Sam. I need to see you start making connections with the students you teach. When I am in your classroom, I sense that you close yourself off to kids. If I can see that, then the students can obviously sense that as well. You need to change that."

"What advice can you give me to get where you want me to be Mr. Massina?"

"Here is where you need to start. Please take this the right way, Sam. I am not evaluating you in relation to Mr. Merriman. However, there are many things that you could learn from him. He was the best I had ever seen at making strong, lasting connections with kids. Talk to the people who worked with him. Talk to the kids about him. I think the things that you will hear about him will get you started in the right direction. Please remember, I am not asking you to be Mr. Merriman. In education, we all steal ideas from each other from time to time to become more effective in the classroom. Steal a few pages from Mr. Merriman's book, and then write the rest of the story on your own."

Chapter 15

When Sam finally pulled into his driveway after work, he realized that he couldn't recall any part of the twenty-minute ride home. Since his meeting with Mr. Massina earlier in the day, he was being bombarded with painful memories and fitful thoughts about the future. Part of him was saying, "Just leave and try to start over again somewhere else." Another part, was saying, "Running from the past is useless." He also had to take into account that he loved the Cayuga community. Even though he grew up in the inner city of Rochester, New York, and usually preferred the atmosphere of city life, Cayuga's small, intimate, suburban setting seemed the perfect match for him and where he was in his life. Sam sat in his living room paralyzed with indecision.

By 9:00 p.m., Sam realized that he had not finished preparing his lesson for tomorrow's classes on the Holocaust novel, *Night*. He forced himself to put aside his dilemma for the time being with the thought that being unprepared for class tomorrow was not going to solve his problem. In front of him on his kitchen table he laid out his laptop and several other resources he was using to prepare his lesson. In class, several days before, Sam gave a pre-test on the Holocaust and realized that the majority of his students lacked basic background knowledge on the subject. So before delving into the novel with them, he was going to spend several lessons discussing and analyzing historical documents leading up to the Holocaust. Sam was going to start with a general discussion of the relationship between World War I and World War II, then end the period analyzing some quotes from Hitler's autobiography, *Mein Kampf*. Sam had found an old tattered copy of the book in the school's library and took it home. When he opened up the book, he noticed that written inside the front cover was, *Jim Merriman 122 Chapin Street (555-3819)*. Just below his name, address, and phone number was the artwork of a small child in crayon depicting a butterfly.

For the very first time since he discovered Jimmy's death, it suddenly hit Sam that his best friend in life was dead. Sam had spent so many years trying to emotionally detach himself from his past that he initially reacted to Jimmy's death as though he was just an acquaintance from the past. However, the knowledge that Jimmy once held this book, had a home, and probably had a family, sent him rocketing back to the bygone days of his childhood. Jimmy was *never* an acquaintance to him. In fact, the first time he met Jimmy, he felt like he had known him his whole life. The feeling of sadness and dread that he felt in his heart when he saw Jimmy being taken away by the paramedics at the baseball field twenty-four years ago came rushing back to him. Only this time it was much different. There was no way to bring Jimmy back—he was gone forever. Sam suddenly missed him badly.

Sam had the book in his right hand and ran his left hand across Jimmy's handwriting and down to the drawing of the butterfly. He could still feel the waxy texture of the crayon left behind by a child who was most likely Jimmy's son or daughter. Sam stared at the phone sitting on the kitchen table thinking to himself, "Should I dial the number?" Sam set down the book, picked up the phone and dialed 5-5-5-3-8-1-9. After letting the phone ring six times, he decided to give up, and just before he hit the *End* button, he heard the voice of a young girl say, *"Merriman's residence—may I ask who's calling?"*

Sam stammered for a moment and said, "This is an old friend of Jimmy's … would I be able to speak to Mrs. Merriman."

"Sure," the young girl said, "Mom there is a friend of Daddy's on the phone!"

In the background Sam could hear a woman's voice directing her children to get ready for bed; then her voice came on the line, "Hello, this is Linda Merriman."

"Mrs. Merriman, this is an old friend of Jimmy's. My name is Samuel Amonte."

There was no reply to Sam's statement. Sam wasn't sure she heard him or just hung up the phone. Sam finally said, "Hello. Mrs. Merriman are you still there?"

She replied in a near whisper, "Sam ... Sam Amonte?"

"Yes, I knew your husband," Mrs. Merriman cut him off in mid-sentence.

"My God Sam, where are you?"

"I am living in town—I am about fifteen minutes away."

"Oh Sam, please, you have to come over right now."

"Mrs. Merriman, I am not sure ..."

Mrs. Merriman pleaded with him. "Please Sam you have to come over—it's 122 Chapin Street ... Please?"

"I guess I could—I'm about 15 minutes away." Sam replied.

"Thank you so much Sam; the girls and I will be waiting."

Chapter 16

Sam smiled when he pulled into the driveway of the Merrimans. Even though it was in a totally different town and nearly a quarter of a century later, Jimmy's house looked strikingly similar to the houses in their old neighborhood. His house was a modest two and a half-story house with an attic and a beautiful front porch. When Sam stepped on to the front porch, the yellow porch light bathed the area with a warm glow that reminded him of the many evenings when he would sit on his own front porch and watch the world go by. As he stood on the porch appreciating memories of those simpler times, he saw a tiny face flash from behind the sidelight curtain. Seconds later, the front door opened, and in front of him stood a five year-old girl in Barbie pajamas with blond hair and blue eyes who asked, "Are you Sam?"

Sam hesitated for a moment because he was struck by the fact that she was the spitting image of Jimmy. Sam finally replied, "Yes I am."

Before either of them said another word, the little girl buried her face into Sam's stomach and grabbed him around the waist so hard that it nearly took his breath away. Sam, taken totally by surprise, raised his arms and uncomfortably patted the girl on the back. Sam then heard the sound of rushing feet and looked up to see a woman in her mid-thirties, with short blond hair, blue eyes, jeans, a hooded sweatshirt, and bare feet racing down the stairs with two other young girls trailing behind. As the woman came closer to Sam, she reached out her arms and held him close as tears began to stream down her face. She then gently kissed him on the cheek, and softly whispered into his ear, "Thank you Sam. Thank you for all you have done for our family."

Sam was taken aback by this unexpected outpouring of familiarity and affection by Jimmy's family. Sam thought he would be walking into their home as a stranger. However, all of the Merriman girls acted as if they had known him their whole lives.

The eldest of the girls, took his hand, led him into the living room and said, "Mom, don't embarrass him. I'm Samantha—why don't you come in and sit down."

Samantha then instructed another girl, whom she called Julia, to go into the kitchen to get coffee, tea, and cookies. Sam was given a very comfortable leather chair to sit in while the three Merriman girls sat directly across from him on the couch. All of them just stared at Sam with big smiles on their faces. When Julia came in from the kitchen with the refreshments, Mrs. Merriman made more formal introductions.

"I'm Linda, Jim's wife, and these are our three daughters. Samantha is our oldest, and she is thirteen. Julia is our middle child, and she is ten. And last, but not least, this is Hannah, she is five."

Hannah looked over to Sam and said, "Would you like one of the cookies I made?"

Sam responded, "I would love to try one of your cookies, Hannah. Thank you."

Samantha said, "Sam, can I pour you some tea or coffee?"

"Tea would be great Samantha—thank you."

Julia then said, "Would you like honey and lemon with that Sam?"

"Both sound delicious Julia—thank you."

Sam reached down and took a bite of his cookie and when he looked up, all four of them were staring at him intently. As Sam sat there, he felt something that he had not experienced for a very long time—he felt at home. These four strangers that he had just met moments ago gave him a feeling of belonging that the hundreds of people and numerous cities and towns could not give him over the last 24 years.

Sam and the Merrimans talked effortlessly for the next hour and a half. Sam heard all about the girls' hobbies, interests, and favorite books. Sam also found out that Linda and Jimmy had moved to town 19 years ago when Jimmy obtained his teaching position at Cayuga. This was their first house, and Linda said that she would never move out of this home because of the amazing memories they had here together. Linda paused for a moment after that statement and looked as if she was going to cry. The girls immediately noticed this and reached out to comfort her. Linda, wiping tears from her eyes said, "They take real good care of me."

After talking for a little while longer, Linda told the girls that it was time for them to go to bed. All the girls came over to Sam, kissed him on the cheek and said, "Thank you." Sam told each of them how great it was to meet them and that he hoped to see them again soon.

When the girls were settled upstairs, Sam asked Linda to tell him all about Jimmy's life since he left town. Linda talked for over an hour and explained to Sam how Jimmy had gone on to college, met her there, married her, and finally became a teacher. She also told Sam how hard it has been for her and the girls these past couple of months without Jimmy. Sam shared memories of his childhood with Jimmy and filled Linda in about what had been going on in his life over these many years, and the recent trouble that he was having at Cayuga. Linda couldn't believe how life's circumstances had brought Sam to Jimmy's school. There was great comfort in her knowing that Sam was currently teaching her husband's students. When Sam was done telling Linda about his life experiences, she looked at Sam and said,

"Jimmy searched for you for many, many years after you left. Several times he came close to finding you, but in each case you had moved along to another place. Sam, you know that he loved you and cared about you very much. He even kept in touch with your mother all these years. She told him that she only received an occasional letter from you saying that you were okay, and you loved her. Why did you have to leave Sam? Your mother, grandmother, and Jimmy were devastated when you left."

"Linda, staying there was going to just bring misery and unhappiness to the people I loved." Sam replied. "I cared too much about them to stay."

Sam started to become noticeably uncomfortable and agitated. He didn't want to relive this right now. With his emotions getting the best of him Sam blurted out, "Sometimes I wish I never would have—" Sam immediately stopped himself because he realized what he was about to say—maybe he never should have saved Jimmy on that day.

Linda realized what he was about to say and looked at Sam in disbelief. Linda said to Sam, "Have you been walking around all these years thinking you had done something wrong? Do you really regret saving Jimmy's life?"

Sam said, "No, no Linda, I don't regret it. I didn't mean to say that. I meant—"

Linda immediately cut Sam off. "You don't get it, do you Sam?"

"Please don't be mad Linda; you have all treated me so wonderfully tonight—"

Linda interrupted him again, "Of course we treated you wonderfully Sam. We love you. We love you as much as Jimmy loved you. I didn't tell my girls how to act towards you tonight. What you saw from them tonight was sincere love and gratitude. Jim talked to them often about you. What did each of the girls say to you tonight as they went to bed? Each of the girls said, 'Thank you'. They weren't thanking you for coming over to see them tonight, or telling them how good the cookies were, or listening to their stories. They were thanking you for giving them the most precious gift they have ever received or will receive in their lives— you gave them their father. You gave them the love of a father. You gave *me* a wonderful, loving husband to share part of my life with. Yes, I feel the pain of missing him every day and will feel that for the rest of my life, but that pain is so overwhelmed and overshadowed by the goodness and beauty Jim brought to my life that I have no regrets."

Linda continued, "Listen Sam, I can't tell you how to live your life. With love comes pain—that is life. The mistake that you made was that you didn't stay around long enough to give your family time to experience the goodness of your heart to overshadow the pain that *you* feel you created. You need to stop running away from yourself. You have a great opportunity here. Jim's students need you. Jim would have wanted it this way."

"I am not Jimmy, Linda. I can't take care of them the way he did," Sam said.

"Sam, Jim was special, but he was special for many reasons. Most of it had to do with the people who influenced his life; his mother, father, me, his children, *and* you. Yes—*you*. He always talked about how special you were—your understanding, compassion, and goodness. He tried every day to emulate those special qualities he remembered about you. Unfortunately, it seems as though you have run so far away from yourself that you've forgotten what made you special. Jim never forgot, and we will never forget."

Sam knew Linda was right. He had spent too much time and effort undercutting who he was as a person that he became someone he couldn't even recognize any more. He realized that he had spent these past years trying to become someone he thought his father would approve of. It suddenly seemed ironic to him that he had spent 24 years trying to please a man who wasn't even a part of his life: yet did nothing to please the man he faced in the mirror each day. At this point, he did not even know who that young man was that he left 24 years ago.

Linda stood up off the couch and told Sam, "Wait one second, I have something for you."

Linda went into the hall closet and pulled out a box. Out of the box she pulled out a leather-bound diary. Linda placed it in his hand and said, "Most nights, while in bed, Jim would write in this notebook his thoughts from the day at school. He felt it helped keep him focused on the truly important parts of being a teacher. Take this home with you. These are all his thoughts about this year's students and the school year. Maybe Jim can help you to find yourself again and help out his students."

Chapter 17

When Sam arrived home after his visit with the Merrimans, he continued his work on the next day's lesson and finally settled into bed around 12:30 a.m. Although Sam was exhausted, he decided to turn on his nightstand light and open Jimmy's diary. Sam immediately noticed that Jimmy's entries were short and to the point. His diary entries would have made great tweets on a *Twitter* page. Sam randomly opened to a page and read an entry from September 28th:

"Good lesson today; could have been much better though. Next time, divide students into small groups to begin poetry unit. Found out Andrew L. likes progressive rock music—Yes, Rush, Genesis. Noticed their names on his spiral. May try playing Rush's song entitled, "Xanadu" and compare the lyrics to Sam Taylor Coleridge's, "Kubla Khan". Paige absent—out sick again. Check with attendance office tomorrow.

Sam flipped a few more pages ahead and read the entry from October 1st, *"Andrew L. involved in class discussion for first time! Very excited to hear Rush in class. Kids brought up other music/lyrics they would like to hear in class. For future lesson, let students select their own songs to inspire the creation of original poems or vice versa … Alexandra stayed after class. Father moved out of house recently—very upset. Gave her pass to eat lunch with her friends in my classroom tomorrow. Paige in school today—finally. However, had parent note to leave early from class for doctor's appointment.*

Sam read a few more entries and then flipped to the last entry in the diary—the night before Jimmy's death. It read: *"January 26th. Can't wait any longer. Need to talk to Massina. Can't stand by and watch what's happening to Paige. Need to gather documentation together to prepare for the firestorm to come."*

After reading the last entry, Sam suddenly remembered the conversation that he had with Daequan the day before. Daequan was concerned about Paige too, but he uncaringly disregarded what Daequan had to say. Sam feverishly began scanning the diary for any other mention of Paige. As he went through the diary, he found several other entries regarding Paige:

"October 10th. Had first face-to face meeting with Paige's parents, Wendy and Alec Lohrman. Brought up issue of Paige's attendance record. Parents explained Paige has suffered from several ailments since early childhood: multiple ear infections, asthma, celiac disease, and various others. Mother (a physician's assistant and veteran of Iraq War) explained that more serious issues had developed that she could not get into at the time. Father (lawyer, school board president) reserved, by very concerned as well. First child died from Sudden Infant Death Syndrome. Parents very caring and concerned for Paige. Tough situation for whole family. Promised parents I would keep a close eye on Paige."

"October 15th. Alexandra's father moved back into house. Parents seeking counseling. Alexandra doing much better—very relieved. Andrew L. really making strides lately. Noticed him in hallway talking to several classmates. Will encourage him to attend school dance on Friday. Paige showed up to class for first time in a week. Left class to go to nurse—felt faint. Had classmate walk her down to nurse."

"November 9th. Paige has been doing excellent lately. Has not missed a day of school for nearly three weeks. Her affect has been very upbeat and looks as energetic as I have seen her all year. Spoke to her after class—she says she has been feeling great. She said she was a little concerned about her mother and grandmother though. Her mother has been away for several weeks taking care of her grandmother, however, would be coming home soon. Received a wonderful note from Alexandra's parents—thanking me for helping her through the tough times recently."

"November 26th. Did an old-fashioned "show and tell" day with kids before Thanksgiving Recess. Learned a tremendous amount about the interests of kids, their families, and their pets. Saw a whole different side to some of the kids. Plan on doing another before Spring Recess. Paige has been in and out of school the past few weeks. Wasn't here again today. Heard from kids she was in emergency room over the weekend."

"December 3rd. Classes were excellent today. Student PowerPoint presentations were fantastic. Spoke to Mary Wise, the school nurse today. Wanted to find out if she had any documentation regarding Paige's illnesses. No specific documentation from physicians."

"December 17th. ...met with Brian Corwin, Paige's school counselor, and Mimi White, the school psychologist, regarding concerns with Paige. Both confirmed that records indicated that Paige has had a similar history of absences throughout school career—progressively worse over last few years though. I expressed concern that no specific documentation was being provided by parents regarding her absences. Both somewhat unconcerned—'that's the way it's always been' and 'Paige was passing all her classes.' Couldn't help but think if this was another student, would they have reacted differently? Think they are afraid to get involved due to fact that Paige's father is on school board. Arrange meeting with parents after winter recess."

"January 4th. Bad day today. Didn't act in the best interest of the kids. Reacted too personally to lack of homework completion by kids. By fourth class of day, I had it, and took it out on whole class. Jessica W. who is always prepared, didn't have homework today and started to cry during my "talk". Found out later in day her grandmother had passed away the night before. Acted like an ass today. Need to apologize to her and the rest of the class for losing my perspective. Will have an <u>intelligent</u> discussion tomorrow on the benefits of completing homework. Began day meeting with Mr. Massina, Wise, Corwin, White, and Paige's parents. Meeting deteriorated very quickly after I stated

that we have an obligation as professionals to seek proof from a physician that Paige cannot attend school on a consistent basis. Mentioned professional duty to inform Child Protection Services— if necessary. Massina was not happy; others looked like they wanted to hide under the table. Paige's parents stormed out of meeting."

"January 7th. Didn't take very long for details of the Jan 4th meeting to get around the school. I guess I came across as 'uncaring' and 'confrontational'. Can't worry about that, have a professional responsibility to Paige, not my image."

"January 14th. Massina called meeting regarding Paige without parents in attendance. Nurse Wise was given documentation from a physician that Paige has been suffering from fainting spells. Blood work inconclusive. Currently testing for seizures. Has also suffered from various infections over the past several months. Massina warned me that district lawyers were contacted by Paige's father regarding my statements at the last meeting. Politely advised me to back off—he would handle it."

Other than the last entry Jimmy made before his death, Sam did not find any other entries regarding Paige in the diary after January 14th. What did Jimmy discover between January 14th and his death that would lead him to believe Paige was in danger? What was this 'firestorm' that was going to occur? Uneasiness started to creep into his head. A teacher with tenure like Mr. Merriman could handle a firestorm, but what was he going to do as a non-tenured teacher? The man he thought his father wanted him to be would never have even noticed that Paige was in trouble in the first place and most certainly would have disregarded the last entry. The man in the mirror told him something different. Tomorrow, he was going to start asking a few questions, and he had a feeling that Daequan could provide him with some answers.

Chapter 18

"Daequan, can I see you for a moment?" Sam called out as Daequan walked by his classroom.

Daequan who was walking down the hall with Alexandra and Mason told them to go on to lunch without him. Sam closed the door behind Daequan and asked him to sit down. While sitting down Daequan said, "Am I in trouble Mr. Amonte?"

"No, not at all Daequan. As a matter of fact, I would like to apologize."

"Apologize to me Mr. Amonte? Why?"

"Yes to you Daequan. You came to me the other day concerned about Paige, and I basically blew you off—didn't I?"

"Well, yeah, you kind of did."

"That was wrong of me, and I'm sorry. I promise that I'll never do that to you again."

"Don't worry about it."

Sam pulled up a chair and sat in front of Daequan's desk and said, "The other day you said that you were worried about Paige. Tell me what you were worried about."

Daequan looked down at his desk and fumbled with his hands. "Mr. Amonte, I don't think I should say anything now. I talked to Mr. Corwin about it, and he told me that Paige is a very sick girl and I shouldn't talk about what I saw. He said my heart was in the right place, but I shouldn't jump to conclusions because it could end up hurting her in the long run. I told him that I wouldn't say anything to anyone else about it. I kinda walked out of his office feeling stupid for telling him."

Sam encouraged Daequan to tell him more. "Daequan, I know that I have given you absolutely no reason to trust me, but I promise you that whatever you said to Mr. Corwin is not stupid, and I will keep it between us. Listen, how about if I tell you something that I shouldn't. I'm going to put my trust in you."

Daequan looked up from his hands for the first time in the conversation.

"Daequan, I think that something bad could be happening to Paige. I think she could even be in danger."

Sam let the statement hang out there for a few seconds to see how Daequan would react, and then said, "What do you think? And if you don't want to answer, I'll understand Daequan."

Daequan's eyes widened as he leaned forward in his chair towards Sam and said, "Mr. Amonte ... So do I."

Sam's heart dropped momentarily. Part of him was hoping that Daequan would disagree and that somehow Jimmy was mistaken. However, Sam pressed on with the conversation. "Why do you think Paige is in danger, Daequan?"

Daequan took a deep breath, got comfortable in his chair, and began to tell the story. "A few weeks ago, I texted Paige to see how she was doing; she hadn't been in school for over a week. She texted me back saying that she was feeling better and asked if I could come over with Alexandra to visit her that night. After school, I called her and told her that we could come over around 8:00. When we got to her house, she looked really bad. I mean Paige is always sick, but this time she really looked bad. I was surprised that her Mom let us over, but Paige said she begged her mom to let us visit. We spent about an hour talking, listening to music, and updating our *Facebook* pages. Then, all of a sudden, her Mom comes in and said that it was time for Paige to take her medicine. She said that we were going to have to go downstairs for a few minutes. At first, Alexandra and I thought it was a little weird that we had to leave the room for her to take a pill, but we went downstairs like she said. While we were downstairs waiting in the living room, I had to go to the bathroom, so I went back upstairs to use the bathroom. When I walked past Paige's room, I noticed her door was cracked open a little and when I looked inside, I saw her mom with a needle thing in her hand giving Paige a shot."

Sam interrupted Daequan for a moment. "Daequan did you know that Paige's mom works as a physician's assistant in a doctor's office? She probably gives shots all the time. So that's probably not unusual in her house."

"I know Mr. Amonte, but listen to what happened next. Mrs. Lohrman saw me looking in the room and when she realized I saw her, she freaked out on me. She stormed out of the room, shut the door, and started asking me what I was doing upstairs spying on them. I tried to tell her that I just had to go to the bathroom, but she just kept on yelling at me. I kept apologizing to her and telling her I just had to go to the bathroom. Then Paige opened the door to her room and begged her mom to stop yelling. As soon as her mom saw Paige was there, she stopped. All of a sudden, Mrs. Lohrman was acting like nothing ever happened. She put her arm around me and led me down the stairs apologizing the whole way. At the front door, she explained that she had been under a lot of stress with Paige's illnesses and was just really worried about her. I told her that it was okay ..."

Sam said, "From what I heard, their family has gone through a lot the past few years, Daequan. Paige had an older sister that died very, very young."

"I didn't know that. But Mr. Amonte—why would she freak out like that? Does she think I have never had a shot or seen someone get one? So what if I saw her giving Paige a shot? You've got to believe me Mr. Amonte, something weird was going on. There was no reason for her to act like that."

Sam had taught Daequan for several months now, and while Daequan could horse around from time to time, he was a respectful and honest young man. There was no reason for him to lie. Sam believed the story Daequan had told him; however, it certainly was not conclusive evidence that Paige was being harmed.

"Daequan, I want you to do me another favor. I want you to keep this conversation quiet."

Daequan's demeanor instantly went sour and interrupted Sam, "Yeah, I get it Mr. Amonte; Mr. Corwin already went through this with me. I'm just a dumb kid who jumps to stupid conclusions." Daequan rose up from his chair to walk out of the room, but Sam gently grabbed his arm.

"Daequan hold up a minute—I believe everything you are telling me. As a matter of fact Daequan, Mr. Merriman would have believed you as well."

Daequan looked at Sam with a surprised expression, "How would you know how Mr. Merriman felt? You didn't even know him."

"Daequan," he said, "I am going to tell you something that I haven't told anyone here at school; Mr. Merriman and I grew up together. He was my best friend."

"No way!" Daequan said excitedly as he suddenly realized something important, "Oh my God, Mr. Amonte—you're *Sam* aren't you?"

"Yes, that's my first name Daequan," he replied.

"No, you don't understand, Mr. Amonte—Mr. Merriman talked about you all the time. You're *the* Sam?"

Sam had known that someday, somewhere, that question would be asked of him. He had also known exactly how he would respond—he would deny it to the bitter end. However, now that the day was here, he shocked even himself with his reply, "Yes, Daequan … I'm that Sam."

Chapter 19

By the time Daequan left Sam's classroom, they had come to an agreement; Daequan would not mention what happened at the Lohrman's house to anyone else, and Sam would do everything in his power to find out if Paige was being harmed. The possibility that Paige was somehow being harmed by her *own mother* seemed preposterous to him. It simply went against all rational thought. Yet, Daequan's story was the only information that seemed to support the thoughts contained in Mr. Merriman's diary. He was going to have to follow through with this, but Sam realized that he was going to have to proceed with extreme caution.

Sam felt that the most obvious place to start would be to contact Linda Merriman. He hoped that Jimmy may have shared some information with his wife regarding Paige. When Sam talked with Linda that night, she mentioned that Jimmy talked about Paige several times over the course of the school year. Unfortunately, she could not impart any new information beyond what was contained in the diary. So Sam decided that the best course of action was to subtly approach other professionals in the building on the premise that he was simply worried about Paige's attendance.

Sam decided to start with Mr. Corwin. Sam popped in the guidance office during his free period. He pretended that he had other business in the office and just happened to pop his head into Corwin's office.

"Do you have a second Mr. Corwin?" Sam said.

"Sure Sam—come on in, but please call me Brian. You make me feel too old when you call me Mr. Corwin."

"Sorry Brian—I'll remember that from now on," Sam replied.

Sam continued, "I just wanted to stop in and talk to you for a few moments about Paige Lohrman."

Mr. Corwin immediately interrupted, "Her attendance—right?"

"Exactly. How did you know?"

"Well, Sam, I have been Paige's school counselor for two years now, and most of her new teachers approach me about her attendance. My heart goes out to this poor young girl—she has so many medical issues. It seems to be just one thing after another. Just when the doctor's seem to get a handle on one diagnosis, another issue seems to come up. She is an absolutely wonderful young lady—it's just such a shame to see her going through all these medical issues."

"Yeah it is," Sam replied. "I can't imagine being her parents and having to go through all of this with a child."

"Her parents are wonderful. Paige's mother has devoted her life to caring for her: all the doctor's appointments, hospital stays, emergency rooms, and therapy. She cares deeply for Paige. Yes, sometimes she can be a little too overprotective of Paige and lash out at people here, but I guess I would be as well if all those things were happening to my daughter."

Sam agreed that he would probably react the same way, and then thanked Mr. Corwin for his time, "Thanks so much for sharing that information with me. Her parents are lucky to have someone like you looking out for their daughter. Is there anything that I can do at all to help the situation?"

"As a matter of fact you can," said Mr. Corwin as he started searching through a stack of papers on his desk. "I was just notified by district office that we are going to need a tutor to go to Paige's home—she is starting to fall behind in a few classes. Would you be willing to tutor her in English and Social Studies? It pays pretty good money."

"I would love to help out." Sam said. "When do they need me to start?"

"As soon as possible—if you can? Actually, the Lohrmans mentioned your name when they were discussing a tutor—they said that Paige enjoys your class."

"That's nice to know, and thank you for all your help."

As Sam turned to leave, he stopped at the door, turned around, and said, "By the way Brian, I wonder if I could take a look at Paige's records. I would like to get a sense of her strengths and weaknesses as a student over the years. I have not had the opportunity to gauge her true abilities with her being absent so much since I arrived here."

"Sure—see Cindy on the way out, and she will pull her file for you."

To Sam, there was nothing that Mr. Corwin shared that indicated any wrongdoing on the Lohrman's part. In fact, Mr. Corwin, who knew the Lohrmans better than anyone on the staff, seemed to provide ample evidence to support just the opposite. Sam hoped that something in Paige's file would provide him with some answers.

Sam started by looking at Paige's attendance records and medical documentation. Over the years, Paige's attendance record did follow the pattern described in Jimmy's diary. Her early years in school showed that while her attendance record was certainly not exemplary, it did not show an above average absentee rate. However, from grades 6-9, there was a definite change. Paige was missing roughly 50-60 school days a year. This young girl had missed the equivalent of over a year's worth of school in just less than three and a half years. When Sam searched through the file for medical records, he found a relatively small amount of medical documentation for a student who had missed so many days of school. Furthermore, the documentation he did find seemed puzzling. When the school would inquire about Paige's medical condition, they would usually have to send out several letters of inquiry before receiving a response. Then, when the Lohrman's physician responded, it always indicated that they were in the process of diagnosing a certain illness, yet never confirming one. After receiving a physician's letter, Paige's attendance record would improve slightly, and then deteriorate again. When the school sent out several inquiries about the next episode of extended absences, it was followed again by a physician's letter outlining the suspicion of yet *another* illness. However, once again, there was no confirmation of an illness, only the suspicion of one.

Next, Sam began looking at Paige's grades and corresponding comments from her teachers. Paige's grades seemed to be remarkably good for a student who missed so many days of school. However, he did notice that her grades over the past few years were beginning to suffer. The accumulation of so many absences was starting to catch up with her. Teacher comments were consistent: *"Student is a pleasure to have in class."*, *"Student is working to best of her ability."*, *"Student is courteous, respectful, and polite."* and *"Absences affecting student's performance."* Sam could easily see why professionals in the building accepted things as they were—all were following standard protocols, and all expressed compassion and sympathy for Paige and the Lohrman family. Still one thing bothered Sam; why wasn't there one confirmed serious illness in the medical documentation?

Sam sat at his desk staring at the file thinking about that question. He started thumbing through the records again trying to find something he may have missed. Then, Sam remembered something from Jimmy's diary. He went into his brief case and pulled out the diary. He remembered something in one of the entries. He searched through the diary and came to what he was looking for in the November 9th entry:

November 9th. Paige has been doing excellent lately. Has not missed a day of school for nearly three weeks … Spoke to her after class—she says she has been feeling great … Her mother has been away for over several weeks taking care of her grandmother, however, would be coming home soon …" Sam then went to the November 26th entry: "*… Paige was been in and out of school the past* *few weeks. Wasn't here again today. Heard from kids she was in emergency room over the weekend."*

Sam suddenly realized that the only positive entry in Jimmy's dairy regarding the physical and emotional health of Paige occurred when her mother was away from home. Sam began combing over the attendance records again to find any other instances where Paige had not missed school over an extended period of time. Sam found two such instances. One instance occurred during the 2003-04 school year. For a seven-month period, Paige had only missed one day of school. The other instance occurred in the 2005-06 school year. Again, for roughly 7-8 months Paige's attendance was normal. Jimmy's entry alone was not enough to prove that there was a correlation between Paige's health and the proximity of her mother. However, if he was able to find out if Mrs. Lohrman was living outside of the Lohrman home during the periods in 03-04 and 05-06, then he could establish a correlation. Sam couldn't help but think Jimmy had already made that discovery on his own.

In the end, Sam's review of Paige's records were helpful, yet only created more unanswered questions. He hoped that his visit to the Lohrmans to tutor Paige might provide him with the answers he needed.

Chapter 20

"It's very nice to meet you, Mr. Amonte—please come in; Paige is in the den waiting for you," Mrs. Lohrman said as she greeted Sam in the foyer of their home.

"It is nice to meet you as well, Mrs. Lohrman—thank you for giving me the opportunity to work with Paige."

"Please Mr. Amonte, we wouldn't want it any other way—Paige was really happy to know that you would be the teacher who would be tutoring her .... I think she has a little bit of a crush on you," Mrs. Lohrman whispered as she led Sam through the kitchen.

Sam and Mrs. Lohrman entered the den and Mrs. Lohrman said, "Paige, look who is here."

Sam walked over to Paige and shook her hand and said, "Paige, nice to see you again. How are you feeling?"

Before Paige could answer, Mrs. Lohrman immediately answered, "She has been up and down lately, but we are working closely with our physicians to get to the bottom of this. But everything will be okay, right honey?"

"Yes, Mom." Paige answered.

"Well, I am going to let you guys get started working," Mrs. Lohrman said. "Mr. Amonte, do you mind if I work at my desk over at the other end of the room while you are working with Paige. I have been out of work a lot lately caring for Paige, and I have quite a bit of work to catch up on."

"I don't see a problem with that, do you Paige?"

Paige looked at Sam, then her mother, and finally said, "No, I don't mind."

Sam spent one hour tutoring Paige in English and the next hour working on social studies. For that two-hour period, Mrs. Lohrman only left the room twice for a total of about ten minutes. Sam thought that Paige was a wonderful young lady; very bright and articulate, but lacking somewhat in higher-level skills which was probably due to her high absentee rate. Sam was confident that he could get her caught up if he was able to work with her several times a week until the end of the year.

After about two hours, Mrs. Lohrman stood up at her desk and announced that the session was over. She explained that she felt Paige didn't have the strength to complete the full session. Sam rose from his chair, told Paige he would see her tomorrow and walked over to the side of Mrs. Lohrman's desk to shake her hand. As he leaned over to shake her hand, he noticed several pictures of Mrs. Lohrman on the desk in an army uniform. The background in the photograph looked like a desert region— perhaps the Middle East.

"That's right; you served in the military—right Mrs. Lohrman?"

"Yes, the Army Reserve. I was a nurse in the 344th Task Force based out of Fort Tallon. That picture of me here was when I was in the Army medical unit assigned to Abu Ghraib. My job was to provide health care for detainees in Iraq. That was my first deployment. About a year later, I was activated again to Camp Bucca about 350 miles farther south."

"That must have been an incredible experience for you," Sam said.

"They certainly had their challenges. We did the best we could to ensure that detainees received the same level of care as any U.S. soldier serving in the region."

"It must have been tough on you and your family being away from home. How long were you stationed in Iraq?" Sam inquired.

"I was there for just about over a year and a half. I was gone for about seven months during my first deployment in 03-04. Then just a little less than 10 months in 05-06."

Sam stood there stunned and speechless for a moment.

Are you okay, Mr. Amonte?" Mrs. Lohrman asked.

Yes ...Yes, I'm fine. So, I will see Paige again tomorrow at the same time?"

Sounds great Mr. Amonte. Paige will be ready.

Chapter 21

The next day, Sam stood outside his classroom doorway waiting to greet his 8th period class. Even though class was not scheduled to begin for another five minutes, Sam wanted to make sure that he was there to greet each student. Jimmy mentioned frequently in his diary how important he felt it was to greet each student at the door—in a sense welcome them as "guests into his home".

Mr. Merriman often likened each class period to a successful dinner party. His wife Linda teased him when he mentioned this analogy. She would say to him, *"Maybe you should start having your students start calling you Mr. Stewart after Martha Stewart."* When she said that to him, Mr. Merriman would go into his best Martha Stewart imitation and end it with her signature phrase, *"It's a good thing."* Linda loved when he did this imitation because both of them would laugh uncontrollably with him playfully chasing her around the house with whatever kitchen utensil was nearby. His favorite move was to recline on the couch with his shirt off trying to strike his "sexiest" pose and saying, *"C'mon Honey, you know you can't resist this—it's a good thing!"* More often than not, his silly antics worked, and Linda would jump on to the couch smothering him with playful kisses.

Mr. Merriman, who loved to host dinner parties at his home, always said that a successful dinner party starts with careful preparation, delicious food and drink, and the creation of a warm and inviting atmosphere. A successful classroom lesson is very similar.

When preparing for a successful dinner party, a host usually spends a considerable amount time planning and preparing for the event. Perhaps the most important thing for a host to consider are the guests. A good host takes note of the backgrounds, interests, and food concerns of the guests attending the party and creates the menu, seating arrangements, and an overall ambience to ensure that all have an enjoyable experience.

When Mr. Merriman planned a lesson for a class, he always started by considering the make-up of students in the class; their backgrounds, interests, and ability levels. For example, if he was preparing a lesson for a class with a high percentage of special education students, he would not have them spend the entire period independently reading a long, complicated passage followed by numerous questions. He likened that situation to a host serving guests who were allergic to gluten and nuts, lasagna for the main course and peanut butter pie for dessert. While his students would not be hospitalized from such a lesson, they most certainly would learn very little.

However, Mr. Merriman knew that serving the most delicious and delectable meal did not guarantee a successful party if the guests did not feel comfortable and welcomed in your home. The first step in achieving this feeling starts with greeting your guests warmly at the door. The first step in a successful lesson was to meet your student at the classroom door.

Standing at his classroom door, Sam thought about what took place at the Lohrmans the day before. Mrs. Lohrman's deployment to the Middle East correlated with the only instances in Paige's school career that showed a consistent pattern of good attendance. However, this fact, accompanied by the word of a 16 year-old, and a vague diary entry did not constitute compelling evidence that Paige was being harmed by her mother. Sam was going to need more to prove that.

Lost in his thoughts, Sam was startled by the voice of Miss Petrucci. "Mr. Amonte, I see you have taken a page out of the book of Mr. Merriman."

Sam just looked at her puzzled and surprised. Angelina Petrucci taught social studies several classrooms down from Sam. Each day they would exchange "good mornings", and then go on with their day. However, Angelina looked different to him today. She usually dressed smartly, hair up, and donning glasses, but today, "Casual Friday", Angelina looked quite different. Angelina's hair was down, with her long, jet-black locks resting gently upon her shoulders. She was dressed in jeans and a silky blouse that accentuated her figure—a fact that had somehow alluded him up until this time. But it was Angelina's eyes that caused Sam to fumble his words. Angelina's sparkling blue eyes left him speechless. Luckily, Angelina broke the awkwardness, "You're waiting outside for your kids to arrive—right?"

"Yes, Miss Petrucci."

Angelina Petrucci smiled furtively, trying not to make it too obvious to Sam that she knew exactly what he was thinking. "Were you and Jim close, Angelina?"

Angelina looked away forlornly for a moment and said, "Jim was the first person to make me feel welcomed when I came to Cayuga. He took me around the school, introduced me to people, invited me to happy hours, and spent countless hours encouraging and advising me. He was the heart and soul of Cayuga." Then she smiled, and her eyes lit up again, "I loved watching him interact with the kids every day. He was so funny. He somehow found a way to wring every ounce of potential out of these kids. He was a master teacher."

"How long have you been here at Cayuga?" he said trying to contribute something from his end of the conversation.

"This is my tenth year now."

As kids began to fill the hallways, she said, "You know a bunch of us are meeting after work at the *Marriot* for happy hour. Why don't you stop by after work, and I will introduce you to some of the other teachers and aides. There are some really fantastic people here at Cayuga. I promise you will have a good time meeting them."

At this point, Sam would have done anything Angelina asked of him. Finally, Sam gained his composure and looked Angelina straight in the eyes and confidently said, "Angelina, I find it very difficult to say 'no' to you. I'll see you there around five."

Angelina smiled and said, "Well, I will see you there then—Sam."

Sam watched Angelina as she walked away with a huge smile adorning his face. When he turned back around he was surprised by Olivia and Daequan standing at his door, each with laughing eyes and broad smiles on their faces. Daequan was the first to speak.

"Hey Mr. A, having a good day today?" Olivia looked at Sam and giggled.

Sam felt his face get a little flushed and said, "How can I not have a good day knowing I have you two to teach this period, Daequan."

Daequan nodded his head approvingly in a "way to go" fashion and stuck out his fist. Sam responded with a fist pound.

Alexandra was the next to arrive to class. Sam told her how much he enjoyed reading her journal entry last night, and what a wonderful writer she was. Alexandra was so pleasantly surprised by the comment that she could only respond with a simple, "Thanks Mr. A."

Alex followed closely behind, and Sam complimented him on his play in yesterday's baseball game against rival, Edison Tech. Sam told him what a phenomenal arm Alex had and how he reminded him of a great pitcher he knew growing up—Mr. Merriman. Alex couldn't believe that Mr. Merriman was such a great pitcher, but he was even more surprised by the fact that Sam grew up with him. Somehow, the knowledge of Sam and Mr. Merriman growing up together made Alex feel differently about Sam; he didn't seem "just the sub" anymore.

Sam greeted each student until only Andrew Lambert was left. As usual, Andrew and Mrs. O'Brien were the last to arrive. When they approached the door, Sam said, "Mrs. O'Brien—do you think Andrew would mind reading the most interesting essay by a student I have ever read in my career?"

Andrew said, "I'll read for you Mr. A. Whose is it? Olivia's?"

Sam handed the essay to Andrew, and when he looked at the paper, Andrew saw his name written at the top with an "A+" beside it. Andrew and Mrs. O'Brien smiled. Sam placed his hand on Andrew's shoulder and said, "C'mon in Andrew, the class is yours for the next 15 minutes."

Chapter 22

When Sam walked in the Marriot Lounge, he noticed Angelina and twenty-five other people from Cayuga standing at the bar. As soon as he walked in, Angelina rushed over to him, took him by the arm, and walked him over to the Cayuga staff. Angelina took the time to make sure he met each staff member who was there that night. Ordinarily, Sam would feel uncomfortable being introduced to so many people at once, but Angelina helped him feel at ease—at least that was until the introductions were over. So much of his attention was focused on watching Angelina effortlessly work through the introductions, that at the end, he realized he couldn't recall the names of any of the people he had just met. Sam just couldn't seem to take his eyes off her. This impromptu gathering was quickly becoming much more than he had expected.

Initially, Sam accepted the invitation only because he was feeling lonely and thought that Angelina was attractive. He really wasn't expecting too much out of the night; just a friendly get-together with co-workers and maybe the chance to get to know Angelina a little better. However, from the moment he walked into the lounge, Angelina had him on his heels. One moment, he was blown away by her charm; the next, her wit; the next, her beauty.

After everyone from school had left, Sam and Angelina stayed behind and decided to get a table for dinner. It was the first time during the evening that they were able to get the chance to talk alone. The conversation flowed effortlessly about Cayuga, politics, his travels around the country and Angelina's family—that was until Angelina began to ask about his family. For the first time in the night, she could immediately sense that he was uncomfortable with their conversation. Angelina quickly attempted to apologize, but Sam cut her off—

"Angelina, it's okay. Please don't apologize, you haven't done anything wrong. It's just not easy for me to talk about my family."

"I was having such a nice time talking with you Sam; I didn't mean to ruin it."

"You haven't ruined anything Angelina. In fact, this is the best time I have had in a very long time," Sam said while flashing a reassuring smile.

"I'm glad you feel that way. The very first time I saw you come down the hallway, I said to myself, *'Who is that?'* You looked so handsome." Angelina looked away for a moment feeling a little embarrassed for being so forward.

Sam thought carefully before he responded. He wanted to make sure that what he was about to say would come out just right.

"When I came to Cayuga, the only thing I cared about was doing a good job. I wasn't interested in making friends or dating. I didn't take the time to notice anyone—even you. I just kept my head down and plowed ahead. I know your thinking, 'Geez, what a way to return a compliment!' But I'm not finished. When you came up to me today in the hall, you looked incredible—beautiful, sexy—I mean you had me speechless. I couldn't believe that I hadn't noticed you in that way before. Then, tonight ... well ... you've shown me that your beauty runs very deep."

For the next several seconds, not another word was said between them. Sam and Angelina stared into each other's eyes until he slid closer to her, gently grasped her face with both hands, and kissed her softly on the lips.

For the first time in many years, Sam felt like he could express his true self to someone again.

Chapter 23

Sam had not seen Paige for nearly three weeks. The last time he was supposed to tutor her, Mrs. Lohrman answered the door and abruptly dismissed him by saying that Paige was not feeling well enough to see him. He was becoming more and more worried about her because rumors were swirling around the school that Paige was very sick. Many of her friends had not even talked with her for a while. Mr. Corwin had called home frequently to see what was going on, but Mrs. Lohrman shared very few details with him. Sam knew that he was going to have to find a way to see her.

Sam decided that he would call Mrs. Lohrman and tell her that he wanted to drop off some textbooks for her to use with Paige if at some point she felt well enough to complete some school work. At first, Mrs. Lohrman was hesitant, but then she reluctantly agreed to allow him to come over to the house.

When Sam arrived at the Lohrmans, he was surprised to see Mr. Lohrman answer the door. Up to this point, he had never met him. He looked exhausted, but Mr. Lohrman greeted him warmly. "You must be Mr. Amonte—please come in. It is very nice to meet you. Thank you so much for taking the time to come by."

Sam walked into the foyer with his arms filled with textbooks and worksheets for Paige. "It is nice to meet you as well Mr. Lohrman. How is Paige doing? We are all worried about her at school. Is there anything we can do?"

"She has not been doing well as of late, although she seemed to be a little better today. The doctors seem to think that—"

Just then, Mrs. Lohrman hurriedly came walking in from the study. With no greeting, she said, "Are these the materials for Paige?"

"Well, yes they are Mrs. Lohrman. I thought that perhaps I could sit down with Paige and give her some directions on how to complete the assignments I have for her."

"She really isn't up for that today Mr. Amonte—just leave them with me, and I will figure them out."

Mr. Lohrman asked tentatively, "Honey, don't you think Mr. Amonte could just see her for a few minutes? She seems a little better today."

Just then, Paige appeared at the top of the stairs dressed in a sweatshirt and sweatpants. Sam was taken aback by how pale and fragile she seemed. "Mom … can I just see Mr. Amonte for a little bit? Please, I am feeling better today—just for fifteen minutes. I am so behind in school; it would make me feel so much better if I could try to catch up a little." Mrs. Lohrman shook her head from side to side.

"Please Mom?"

"Okay Honey. But just for a few minutes. I don't want you to get overtired."

Sam said, "I promise that I won't stay long Mrs. Lohrman. I will just explain a few of the worksheets, then let Paige get some rest."

Sam and Paige went into the kitchen and sat at the table. Sam went through each of the assignments, while Mrs. Lohrman hovered just outside the kitchen near the foyer. Sam saw a pronounced change physically and emotionally in Paige. She seemed thinner and paler from the last time he saw her. Paige, who always had a vibrant personality, was very sullen. It seemed him as though someone had turned a light off inside of her. He knew she was clearly ill.

In a very soft and weak voice, Paige asked Sam if he wanted something to drink. He told her that he was fine, but she insisted on getting him something from the refrigerator. As she opened up the refrigerator and reached in for a glass pitcher of iced tea, Paige suddenly collapsed. The pitcher shattered on the tile floor scattering pieces of glass and spilling iced tea everywhere. Mrs. Lohrman came running into the kitchen with Mr. Lohrman and screamed, *"Oh my God!"*

Mrs. Lohrman quickly checked over Paige's entire body. Miraculously, Paige was not cut by any of the glass that had shattered. Dazed and drenched in iced tea, Paige asked her mother what happened. Mrs. Lohrman knelt down and held Paige's head in her arms and started yelling at Mr. Lohrman, "I told you she wasn't up to this! I am the only one that understands her medical condition. You and all these doctors have no idea what she is going through!"

Mr. Lohrman went to help his wife lift his daughter from the floor, but she only pushed him away. Sam and he watched Mrs. Lohrman lead Paige carefully up the stairs to her room. Mr. Lohrman slowly and carefully started picking up the pieces of glass. Sam began to help him, and Mr. Lohrman softly thanked him. It took them both at least thirty minutes to clean up the mess. When they were finished, Mr. Lohrman thanked Sam for coming by and helping to clean up.

"Well, if you will excuse me Mr. Amonte, I am going to go upstairs and see how Paige is doing."

"Please tell Paige that I hope she feels better, and she will be in my prayers."

"Thanks, I will tell her Mr. Amonte."

Sam picked up the plastic bag filled with paper towels and glass and told Mr. Lohrman that he would throw it in the outside garbage cans for him. He thanked him again and told Sam that the cans were on the side of the garage.

When Sam opened the lid to the trash can, he lifted out a trash bag that was already lying in there, so he could place the bag with sharp, broken glass at the bottom to avoid someone being injured. However, when he lifted out the first bag, the bottom fell out and the contents fell onto the ground. Tin cans, plastic jars, chicken bones, a baking tin, paper plates, and napkins were strewn all over the sidewalk along the garage. Sam carefully placed down the bag filled with broken glass and began picking up the trash that had fallen. As Sam was bent over picking up the trash, he cut himself on something sharp. Underneath a soiled napkin, he found what had cut him—a small broken medical vile. The vile had cracked, but the label had kept the vile from shattering. As he carefully picked it up to place it back in the trash, he looked at it and could only read the first part of the label—C-o-u-m. Suddenly, Mrs. Lohrman appeared behind Sam.

"What are you doing Mr. Amonte?" said Mrs. Lohrman.

Sam replied, "I'm sorry, I was throwing away the mess from the kitchen for your husband and one of the bags broke open."

Sam hurriedly picked up the rest of the trash and placed the lid on the can. As he walked by her to get to his car, he apologized for what had happened today.

Mrs. Lohrman did not respond and just stared at Sam as he drove out of the driveway. Looking in his rearview mirror, he could see her continuing to stare as he drove down the road.

Chapter 24

Driving home, Sam was both disturbed and upset by what he had witnessed at the Lohrmans. In just a matter of weeks, Paige was just a shell of her former self. Despite Jimmy's diary entries, the attendance records, his talk with Daequan, and what he had personally witnessed in the Lohrman's home, he simply could not wrap his head around the idea that a parent could possibly harm their child. Yes, he had heard about cases of child abuse in his career, but this situation did not fit the profile of abuse that he had witnessed before. The previous cases of abuse were overt: obvious neglect, black eyes, broken bones, witnesses to the abuse, or personal confirmation of abuse by the children themselves. However, this situation was entirely different.

The Lohrmans were respectable members of the community. Mr. Lohrman was president of the school board. Mrs. Lohrman was a nurse and a veteran of the Iraq and Afghanistan wars. As parents, they took an active role in the education of their child and were reported by members of the Cayuga staff as being parents who were deeply concerned with the physical and emotional well-being of their child. As a matter fact, if they were guilty of anything, it would be that they were sometimes overprotective. Sam wrestled back and forth in his mind with these conflicting thoughts as he was driving home.

About ten blocks from his home, Sam slammed on his brakes and brought his car to a sudden, screeching halt. He had been so preoccupied with his thoughts and emotions that he nearly plowed into the back of another vehicle stopped at a red light. Sam looked up and saw the driver of the vehicle in front of him flailing his hands in the air and yelling obscenities at him. Sam rose up both his hands and mouthed the words, "I'm sorry" over and over again to the other driver. After the light turned green, he pulled his car into the nearest parking lot and sat there with his hands and head resting on the steering wheel.

As he sat there, he wished that he could sit down and talk with Jimmy about the situation. He wondered; what information did Jimmy come across that led him to believe that Paige was in danger? Did someone come to him with information? Did Paige share anything with him? Did he personally witness something? Did he possibly share any of his thoughts with another staff member?

Soon memories of Jimmy and his childhood came flooding back to him. He thought about all the great times he had with Jimmy. The hundreds of football, basketball, and baseball games they played in the school playground at #39 School. The times when they would go into Jimmy's basement and take turns playing Jimmy's drum set and a broom air guitar to Led Zeppelin, Rush, and Hendrix albums. All the fun times they had together in class. Sometimes they spent more time laughing with each other in class than learning. Each day in English class of their junior year, they would sit next to each other despite the fact that their teacher's seating chart had them on opposite sides of the room. Every single day they would come into the classroom and sit next to each other and every single day Mr. Janson would say, "Merriman, Amonte—move!"

This went on for five straight months until one day Mr. Janson looked up from his attendance sheet, saw both of them sitting next to each other again and said nothing. This time he just looked up at them and gave them both a wry smile, as if to say, "I admire your persistence boys!" From that day on Mr. Janson always let them sit next to each other. To show their appreciation, Sam and Jimmy actually made it a point to pay more attention in class. Mr. Janson went on to become one of their favorite teachers.

"Junior year ..." Sam said aloud to himself in the car, and then started laughing uncontrollably. The thought of this time period brought him back to the memories of the Junior Prom.

103

Just before the prom, Jimmy received his driver's license and permission from his father to drive the family's brand new Chrysler *Newport*. The *Newport* was the perfect high school car because you could squeeze about six in the back and four in the front. Sometimes more if the situation arose. But on prom night, it was just the two of them alone with their dates making out in a deserted parking lot. Sam remembered Jimmy looking back at him for a second from the front seat while he was kissing his date. Sam knew exactly what he was thinking, "Can you believe it man? I am making out with Ann Marie Mancini!"

By the time the marathon make out session was over, Jimmy was feeling on top of the world. Feeling just a little too full of himself, Jimmy decided to impress the girls with his driving skills and started to do a few doughnuts with the car in the parking lot. Well, somehow, the clunky heel of his platform shoe got wedged underneath the gas pedal, and everyone in the car was getting tossed from one side of the car to the other as Jimmy tried to desperately get the car under control. Somehow, he finally unwedged his foot from the gas pedal, and the car came to a screeching halt. Sam would never forget the scene when the car finally came to a stop. Sweat was running profusely down Jimmy's face. The girls, who spent so much time to look pretty on that night, looked like they had just been tumble dried in a dryer. Their dresses were disheveled, their hair was a mess, and they both looked like they were going to throw up any second. After they dropped off their dates, they both drove home in tears laughing at what had just happened. The last thing Jimmy said to him that night in his driveway was, "Do you think I should call Ann Marie for another date?"

Sam jokingly told him he should lose her number and look into the priesthood or at the very least—buy a new pair of shoes. What Sam wouldn't give to be able to sit with Jimmy again and reminisce about their time together?

Thoughts of Jimmy now drifted to his mother and father. He missed them too. Sam regularly sent letters to his mother because he always wanted her to know that he was doing well. He never wanted his mother to worry, so he always kept his letters upbeat and positive. Despite what had occurred between him and his father, Sam always concluded his letters by asking his mother to tell his dad that he loved him. For the first time in a very long while, Sam actually contemplated calling home.

He reached for his cell phone on the seat and dialed their number. A man answered the phone and said, "Hello", but Sam did not respond. Even though he had not heard this voice for many, many years, he immediately recognized the voice as his father's. His father once again spoke, "Hello, who is this?"

Sam did not respond again. After a few seconds of silence, Sam heard his father say, "Sam, is it you?" Startled, he immediately ended the call and threw the phone back on the seat. Tears began to well up in Sam's eyes. He wanted so desperately to answer his father, but he could not. He sat there for a few moments and once again picked up the phone and dialed.

This time Sam spoke, "Hi, it's Sam ... Yes, I am okay ... Do you think that I could come over and see you?"

Chapter 25

Sam pulled into the driveway and took a moment to collect himself. As he closed his car door, he looked at the house and noticed that it had seen better days. When he stepped onto the front stoop, his heart started to beat faster, and he began to wonder if he was doing the right thing. Even though his instincts told him to turn around and leave, and that maybe it was too soon, he reached out and rang the doorbell.

As soon as the door opened, he knew that he made the right choice. The sight of Angelina at the door immediately lifted his spirits. As he stepped into her house, she immediately sensed that he was upset.

"Sam ... What's wrong?" said Angelina as she tried to instantly read his mind and facial expression.

"Listen, Angelina ... I know that we just met, but I just needed to talk to someone."

Angelina was concerned and happy at the same time. She had not been able to stop thinking about Sam since the happy hour. The fact that he was coming to her made her realize that the night might have been special for him as well. However, she could tell that something was deeply upsetting him.

"Come in and sit down with me."

Angelina took Sam by the hand and led him into the living room. They sat down upon the couch together, and Sam spoke first.

"I think that one of my students is in danger."

"Which one?"

"Paige Lohrman."

"The girl who has been out of school for a while?"

"Yes. Do you know her?"

"No, but I heard a few of the kids talking about how sick she is. They say that she is out of school a lot. Is she that ill, Sam?"

"I think that she is seriously ill."

"What's wrong with her? Does she have a serious disease?"

"Angelina, I know that you are going to find this hard to believe, but ..." Sam paused because he still found it hard to believe himself.

"What Sam? What's wrong with her?"

He looked at her and said, "I think her mother is poisoning her."

Angelina looked at Sam hoping that this was some kind of a joke, but she could tell that he was dead serious.

"I don't understand Sam. Why would you think this? Did someone tell you this?"

Sam rose to his feet and paced around the room for nearly an hour as he told her the entire story. Angelina sat there stunned—she could barely believe what she was hearing. When Sam was done explaining the situation, Angelina's face was pale. She had taught long enough to know that this situation was fraught with danger on many different levels. First and foremost, the life of a child could be at stake. Second, Sam's professional career would clearly be on the line. A non-tenured teacher accusing the wife of the president of the school board of child abuse—would be a career killer. If Sam was wrong, or could not provide solid proof—he would never teach again.

"What I just cannot get my head around—", Sam said, "is the fact that it is her *mother* that is doing this to her. I am not so naïve to think that child abuse doesn't occur in this world, but this just doesn't fit anything that I have ever heard or read about child abuse. Aren't there supposed to be visible bruises, black eyes, burn marks, something? How can she being doing this? My mother would give her life for me. She would have done anything to protect me from physical or emotional pain."

"You're right Sam—it seems crazy, but I do remember reading about a situation like this when I was taking an abnormal psychology class in college. There was this psychological abnormality we discussed where the parent, usually the *mother* I believe, purposely makes up stories about their child being ill as a way to get attention."

"But this is not a fictitious illness. I saw her Angelina; she is sick, very sick."

"There's more to it though. I think I recall there being various degrees of this illness. I think in some cases it can result in the death of the child."

"What is the name of the psychological condition?"

"It was something like—Munch... Munchenberger's? ... Something German sounding like that ... No—wait—Munchausen's. Munchausen's by Proxy!"

"I have never heard of that." said Sam. "Can I use your computer to look it up online?"

"Come with me. My computer is in the back room." answered Angelina.

Within minutes, they had found a medical website on Munchausen's Syndrome by Proxy. Sam read the site furiously and with each passing fact, he became more and more sickened by what he read. Switching off between reading silently and aloud, he read aloud all the information that paralleled the circumstances surrounding Paige.

"Chronic MSBP is characterized by the constant pursuit of attention through the harming of another individual."

"MSBP is a psychological disorder characterized by a pattern of behavior in which someone, usually a mother, induces physical ailments upon another, usually her child."

"In 98% of the cases, the mother is responsible."

"Mother attempts to gain attention and recognition for herself by putting on the public façade of a dedicated and loving mother. She shows compassion and devotion to her child by

108

giving up much or all of her time to constantly take them to medical professionals."

"Mother usually has medical knowledge or medical background."

"A history of sudden infant death syndrome in siblings may be present."

"Illness only appears or becomes graver in the presence of the parent. Symptoms disappear in the absence of the perpetrating parent, but resume with the reintroduction of that same parent."

"In extreme cases the parent may resort to measures such as suffocation, inducing vomiting with ipecac, removing blood from the child, or poisoning with substances such as hydrocarbons, salt, imipramine, insulin, and *Coumadin*."

Sam stopped reading immediately and said, "Angelina—did you hear that? Coumadin—that's what I found in the garbage."

"Oh my God Sam!" Angelina responded.

Sam continued reading. "Another sign of MSBP is the mother's righteous indignation when confronted by a doctor with their fictitious accounts of the child's medical history or of inducing symptoms in their child. They will sometimes resort to threatening malpractice lawsuits, or even causing the child to become deathly ill to prove to physicians that she was right about the child's condition."

"MSBP claims the life of 9% of children that fall victim to it. 75% of the morbidity cases occur in a hospital setting."

The facts were sobering to the both of them. Angelina asked Sam what he was going to do next. Sam replied, "I am going to call Child Protection Services."

"Sam, I am tenured, let me make the call," Angelina pleaded.

"I am not going to put you in that position Angelina. I am Paige's teacher. I know the details of the situation. I am convinced that I am right on this, and whomever I speak to at CPS has to hear the conviction in my voice."

"I understand that Sam, but do you understand that you are accusing the school board president's wife of child abuse. If something goes wrong, they will make sure that you never teach again. Are you 100% convinced that you are right?"

"Angelina, if I am wrong and act upon this, I lose my job. If I am right, and do nothing, then an innocent child could die. If that occurred, I couldn't live with myself."

"Are you going to tell anyone else about this? Angelina asked.

"I am going to see Corwin tomorrow morning before school starts. I have never contacted CPS before in my career. I am not too sure what to do. I would imagine that he has been involved with CPS."

"Do you want me to go in with you?"

"No. I don't want you involved in this at school. Do you understand me? If anything bad happened to you because of this, it would make this entire situation even more unbearable. Please promise me that you will not get involved in this?

"I promise Sam."

Chapter 26

"Mrs. Lohrman?" said Mr. Corwin as he nearly fell back in his chair.

"Yes, Brian. Mrs. Lohrman," Sam said.

"Sam, you can't be serious, the Lohrmans. I've been Paige's guidance counselor for years. I know them well. I've sat in countless meetings with them. In all my years at this job, I have never come across a more devoted set of parents. You have to be mistaken."

Sam felt compelled to once again explain all of the key indicators of Munchausen's By Proxy and how they mirrored what he had experienced with the Lohrmans. Despite all of this, Mr. Corwin still remained unconvinced.

"Listen Sam, I understand and appreciate your concern for Paige, but it's very easy to read a list of symptoms and mistakenly assign the disease to a person or situation. Haven't you ever heard the stories of how first year medical students start to believe they have many of the various diseases they are studying? This poor family lost a child at a very young age. She's a nurse. Wouldn't it be natural for Mrs. Lohrman to seem a little overly protective and want to take an active role in the care of the only child she had left?"

"Brian, I know it's not easy to believe, but I am not some rookie teacher jumping to wild conclusions. I didn't just come across an article on Munchausen's and search around for a family to apply it to. I knew there was something seriously wrong at the Lohrmans even before I discovered there was a name for this disorder. I am telling you Brian—Paige is in serious danger!"

"For God's sake Sam, she is a war veteran. She has put her life on the line for her country. She's a devoted mother. Mr. Lohrman is a respected member of the school board and entire

Cayuga community. Don't you think he would know if his wife was poisoning his child? I think you are making a big mistake."

When Mr. Corwin had finished what he wanted to say, he waited for Sam to respond. Sam sat there for a few moments staring out of the office window. When he finally broke his gaze, he looked at Corwin and said, "Brian, I need the phone number for Child Protection Services and the appropriate paperwork to fill out."

Mr. Corwin smiled wryly while shaking his head as he got up from his desk and walked over to his file cabinet. When he came back to his desk, he handed a blank Child Abuse Report Form to Sam and briefly explained what he could expect during the phone call. Sam thanked him and walked towards the door. Before he left, Mr. Corwin said one last thing to him.

"Sam, you need to talk to Massina as soon as possible. Also, now listen to me—whatever you do, do not sign the form at the bottom. All reports to CPS can be anonymous unless you sign the report form at the bottom stating that you would like to be made aware of the disposition of the case. If you sign the form at the bottom, the Lohrmans could possibly find out that it is you. You could get in a lot of trouble."

"But if I don't sign, how will I know if Paige is being protected?"

"You have to trust the system Sam."

Sam walked back to his classroom and looked over the form entitled, *Report of Suspected Child Abuse or Maltreatment*. Sam still had an hour before his first class, so he decided to get started on it as soon as possible.

The report was fairly straightforward. There were three required sections to be filled out. The first section, *Subjects of the Report*, required him to state information about the child or children involved, adults' responsible, and alleged subjects in the household. The second section was called *Basis of Suspicion*, and contained a list of all different types of abuse or maltreatment. There were twenty-three types listed ranging from emotional neglect, educational neglect, abandonment and lack of supervision to burns, scalding, fractures, bruises, and fatality. The box that Sam checked was called "*poisoning/noxious substances*". The most important part of the report was also contained in this second section. This subsection required the reporter to: "*State the reasons for the suspicion, including the nature and extent of the child's injuries, abuse, or maltreatment and any evidence or suspicions of parental behavior contributing to the problem.*" Sam spent nearly forty-five minutes on this subsection recounting in writing why he felt Paige was being abused by her mother.

The last section of the report contained the space where the reporter of the abuse could sign his name if he wanted to be updated on the status of the case. Sam paused briefly, and then signed the form.

Upon finishing the form, his first students of the day began to filter into his classroom. For the next several hours, Sam taught his classes, but found it very difficult to concentrate on the delivery of his lesson. As soon as he was done teaching for the day, he was going to go down to see Mr. Massina and let him know that he was going to call CPS. On his way there, he noticed some of his students clustered around a locker. As he reached the locker, he saw that Olivia was at the center of the crowd crying. Sam saw Daequan and said, "What's wrong Daequan?"

"Mr. Amonte ... it's Paige ... she's in the hospital."

"What's wrong with her?"

"She's in a coma."

Sam grabbed Daequan by the shoulders and pulled him square to his face.

"Where is she Daequan? What hospital is she in?

"We heard that she was at Highland Hospital."

Sam let go of Daequan and sprinted back to his room to grab his keys and then down to the main office. He told Mrs. Gillette that he had an emergency and had to leave early. He was already out the main doors before Mrs. Gillette could respond.

Chapter 27

"I'm here to see a patient—Paige Lohrman?" said Sam to an elderly woman at the hospital information desk.

She tapped away at the computer keys and said to him, "Sir, she is in the ICU. Are you a member of the family?"

"Yes, I am. Can I see her?"

"Take the elevators to the left to the fifth floor and follow the yellow line and look for signs that say ICU."

Sam thanked her and walked hurriedly to the elevators. Upon reaching the ICU, he was immediately stopped by a nurse at the center desk.

"Can I help you?"

"I am here to see Paige Lohrman."

From the center desk, Sam scanned each of the rooms to see if he could find out which room she was in. The last room he looked in gave him his answer. There, through the open door, he saw Paige lying in a hospital bed. Instantly, he felt as though he was going to vomit. To him, it looked like every conceivable life saving device was attached to her.

"Sir, are you a member of the immediate family. Sir? Sir? I'm afraid that she cannot—"

Sam didn't hear a word she said. He just walked towards Paige's room, transfixed on her face. He could not believe that this once beautiful, vibrant, and innocent young girl was the same person he was now looking at in the hospital bed.

"Hey, you can't go in there!" the nurse called out.

Without remembering a single step, Sam found himself standing at her bedside. Intense waves of nausea, guilt, and rage came over his body. For the first time since reading Jimmy's diary entry about Paige, it all became so clear to him. He thought to himself, "How could I let this happen? Why did I wait so long to do anything about this? Of course it was Mrs. Lohrman. It was all there laid out in front of me, yet I chose to proceed with caution. Now look at her!" He wanted to grab Mrs. Lohrman by the throat and make her pay for this.

Then a man's voice drew him out of his thoughts, "Mr. Amonte? What are you doing here? How did you hear?" The man's voice was Mr. Lohrman. He had just come back from meeting with Paige's neurologist and the news was not good.

"Mr. Lohrman—what's, what's wrong with her?"

"She's in a coma. Preliminary signs are pointing to intracranial bleeding. It's not good ..." Mr. Lohrman's speech trailed off into an almost inaudible mumble. Sam could only make out a few phrases,

"I don't understand ... Why didn't they see this coming? ... My beautiful girl."

Sam walked over to Mr. Lohrman and grabbed his arm to get his attention. Mr. Lohrman slowly lifted his head and looked him in the face. Sam did not mince words.

"Mr. Lohrman, listen to me carefully. It's your wife. There is something wrong with her. She's responsible for this."

The words fell upon Mr. Lohrman like a slap to his face. Mr. Lohrman looked as though he was awakened from a dream. "What did you say?" he said.

"Your wife did this to Paige; she is poisoning her."

Mr. Lohrman instantly became enraged and grabbed two fists full of Sam's shirt, hurling him into the hospital room door. Already leery of Sam's presence, and having witnessed the confrontation, the head nurse immediately called security for help. Sam had not expected Mr. Lohrman to react with such rage.

As Mr. Lohrman continued to violently shake him, Sam realized that he needed to defend himself. With one quick move, he forcefully thrust his forearms upward, broke Lohrman's hold, spun him around and bear hugged him against the wall. While pinning him against the wall, Sam said, "Listen to me—" Mr. Lohrman tried to wriggle away, but Sam had too strong a hold on him.

"Your wife is responsible for this. She has been injecting Paige with Coumadin. This caused the intracranial bleeding. You've got to stop her!"

With the side of his face pushed against the wall and teeth clenched, Mr. Lohrman shouted, "You son of a bitch—let me go!"

Just then, Sam felt the hands of a security guard prying his hands off Mr. Lohrman while he watched another struggling to restrain Mr. Lohrman from assaulting Sam again. Soon, two other guards were on the scene to escort Sam from the ICU. As he was being escorted out, Sam heard Mr. Lohrman screaming, "You'll never teach again you son-of-a-bitch!"

On the way out, Sam pleaded with the security guards to let him speak to Paige's physician, but the guards refused to allow him to remain in the hospital and threatened to arrest him if he did not leave immediately.

When Sam arrived home, he immediately contacted Child Protection Services. A week ago Sam would have been nervous making the call. The gravity of the situation was undeniable—the life of a girl and the lives of an entire family were in the balance. However, on this day, he knew with absolute certainty that his actions were justified. All throughout the call, he couldn't stop thinking that it might all be too late. Why didn't he just act upon this earlier?

The phone call went smoothly because Sam had the foresight to fill out the paperwork ahead of time in tremendous detail. The CPS investigator assured Sam that they would investigate the matter within 24 hours. At first, he felt reassured that they would act so quickly. However, after he hung up the phone, anxiety and dread crept into his consciousness. As he lay upon his bed staring at the ceiling, he realized that the fate of Paige's life now rested in the hands of a government bureaucracy. Yes, they would investigate within 24 hours, but what did that mean? Would they contact Paige's parents first? If they did, would this give Mrs. Lohrman time to cover her tracks, or even worse, do something drastic? At what point would the doctors be notified? Once notified, tests would have to be run and how long would that take? Many other questions raced through his mind, but the last one was the most sobering. Even if the CPS investigators and doctors performed their jobs at the utmost level of professionalism, skill, and compassion, would it already be too late? Has there already been too much damage done for her to even survive the next 24 hours?

Sam was not willing to wait to find out the answer to this question.

Chapter 28

Sam awoke at dawn the next morning. He had spent the rest of the previous night trying to think of a way to save Paige. He knew he had to go to the hospital and save her. He was not going to let her die. Yet, he also knew that it was not going to be easy getting back into the ICU. If he was recognized by someone from the previous day, security would be called in an instant. He was also sure that the hospital staff would be on guard looking out for anyone who was not family that wanted to see Paige. However, Sam was prepared to do anything to get into Paige's room. He was prepared to forcibly enter the ICU and barricade Paige's door if he had to. The problem was he had to get close enough to do it.

As Sam was getting ready to leave for the hospital, there was a knock at his door. When he opened his front door, to his shock and surprise, he found Andrew, Olivia, and Daequan on his porch. Andrew was the first to speak, "We need to talk to you Mr. A."

"Guys what are you doing here? It's 6:30 in the morning. How did you know I lived here?"

"Daequan told us why Paige is in a coma."

Sam and Daequan's eyes met and Sam could see the same level of intensity and conviction in his eyes that he felt himself.

"We have to do something to save her Mr. A."

"Guys, I am going to the hospital right now to do something. I am going to take care of this. I am not going to let her be harmed anymore. You guys just go on to school and I will see you 8th period."

Daequan spoke next. "Mr. A, let us come with you—we want to see her. We heard that she may die. We care about her and want to help her. We went to see her last night, and they wouldn't let us near her. There was even a security guard outside

118

of the ICU. He asked all of us our names and said no one but family could see her. They wouldn't even allow us to leave a note or flowers. What is going on? Why would they have a security guard posted? Is the security guard there to protect Paige from her mother?"

"Listen guys—I can't tell you anything right now. You just have to trust—"

Andrew became extremely agitated; Sam had never seen him like this before. "Mr. A what are you trying to protect us from? We know what is going on. We're not stupid. We are her friends. You are not the only one who cares about her. I know you want us to trust you and we do, but why can't you trust us? Let us help you!"

All three of them looked at Sam and stood there in silence waiting for his response.

Sam took a deep breath and said, "Come inside."

Sam briefly explained to them what he had found out and what had occurred at the hospital the previous day. He told them that he could help her if he could get a few minutes alone with her.

"Mr. A—there's no way you are going to be able to get in to see her." said Olivia. "The security guard is not going to let you near her."

"I know a way he can get in to see her," Andrew said.

For the next fifteen minutes, Andrew explained in clear detail what they could all do to get Sam in to see Paige. When they settled on a plan of action and all were clear of their roles, Olivia said to Sam, "Mr. A—if we do get you in to see her, what are you going to do?"

He responded, "You asked me to trust all of you. Now you trust me. Just give me a couple minutes alone with her and everything will be alright."

Chapter 29

They decided to enter the hospital in small groups and meet outside the elevators on the third floor where the ICU was located. Olivia and Daequan entered the hospital first and took the stairs to the fifth floor. Sam and Andrew entered last. Andrew took his non-motorized wheelchair to the hospital and instructed Sam to push him through the hospital. Andrew knew that a person in a wheelchair was never questioned like most other people. In fact, he knew most people went out of their way to help a handicapped person.

The plan was for Olivia and Daequan to first try and enter the ICU as a diversion. As they walked several yards ahead of Sam and Andrew, they noticed that there was no guard standing outside of the ICU. Both were encouraged by this fact. Daequan pushed the electronic door opener to enter the ICU, while Sam and Andrew waited outside looking through the small door window. Olivia and Daequan walked down a short corridor that led into a common area that contained a nurse's station in the center with individual ICU rooms surrounding it. For a moment, neither of them saw anyone in the common area until they fully entered it and spotted a security guard talking to one of the nurses just outside of a kitchen area off the ICU and an elderly, Hispanic woman mopping the floor. As soon as they spotted them, their hearts started beating faster. Olivia felt like running, but Daequan reached out and held her hand as they approached the nurse and security guard.

"Kids, I am sorry, but you cannot be here." said the nurse.

Daequan responded, "Excuse me ma'am, we apologize for being here so early, but we were hoping to see our friend Paige Lohrman before school. We talked to her mother last night and she said that we might be able to see her today. We are all so worried about her and wanted to at least drop off these flowers and this card from everyone at school."

The nurse said, "I can make sure that she gets the flowers and card, but you cannot see her. Her parents just went down to get some breakfast, I will make sure that they get the card and flowers. Now you kids are going to have to—"

Just then, Sam and Andrew appeared in the common area. Andrew was slumped down in his chair trying to look as weak and fragile as possible. Sam wearing a baseball cap wheeled him in gingerly while keeping his head down and pretending to comfort and console Andrew as they walked in.

"Don't' worry—" Sam said to him. "I'm sure that you'll be able to see her."

The sight of Sam and Andrew drew the attention of the nurse and the security guard. Their sudden appearance clearly made the nurse more agitated because she immediately rushed over to them and barked,

"You cannot be here. As I told these other children, no one is allowed to see her. This is an ICU, and the family has given us strict orders."

While the security guard and nurse were speaking to Sam and Andrew, Olivia looked into the last room to the right and saw Paige lying in bed with what seemed like countless wires and tubes going in and out of her. Olivia immediately started to cry at the sight of Paige's nearly lifeless body. Olivia ran over to Paige's door and pressed her tear stained face upon the window. Seeing Olivia crying at the door, the security guard rushed over to her to prevent her from entering. As the security guard got closer to Olivia, she started to back up from the door, and said, "Leave me alone. Don't touch me. I want to see her!"

Olivia had the security guard following her all the way to the other side of the ICU as another nurse appeared and tried to calm her down. Daequan rushed over and started to yell at the security guard to leave Olivia alone.

When Andrew saw that Olivia and Daequan had the security guard occupied, he immediately went into action. Suddenly, he slumped over in his chair, with his face nearly touching his knees. Sam leapt from behind the chair, went down on one knee, and grabbed Andrew's shoulders. Making sure that he cushioned Andrew's fall, Andrew purposefully rolled out of the wheel chair and lay motionless on the floor. Sam yelled at the nurse to help him, as the Hispanic orderly dropped her mop and rushed over to help as well.

In the midst of the chaos, Sam cautiously made his way over to Paige's room, and then quietly opened the door. While Daequan was engaged with the guard, Olivia watched Sam enter Paige's room. Through the window, she saw a bright light begin to form and slowly intensify near Paige's bedside. Her eyes held an unwavering focus on the light.

Like the interaction between the sun and the moon during a total solar eclipse, she watched her teacher's body slowly move in front of the intense light until it became as black as night. For several seconds, the light, like the sun's majestic corona, emanated from the outline of Sam's body. As Sam reached for Paige's face, the light began to move off to the side and became so intensely bright that Olivia had to shield her eyes. As the light began to dim, it slowly transformed into the shape of a small man.

Olivia suddenly became aware that the sound of all the commotion at the nurse's station turned to silence. One by one, each person at the nurse's station had disengaged from their situation and focused their attention to Paige's hospital room. All had become transfixed upon the light and stared in silence.

When the light slowly dissipated, everyone could clearly see Sam in Paige's room. Yet surprisingly, the nurses and guard made no movement towards the room. When the light disappeared, Sam walked from Paige's bedside and exited the room. No one made an attempt to stop him. The Hispanic woman stood there motionless as he approached, then uttered something in Spanish and made the sign of the cross as he passed by. While still lying on the floor, Andrew looked up at Daequan and Olivia and smiled. The guard and the nurses simply watched

Sam walk by and nonchalantly leave the ICU. Shortly thereafter, all of the kids followed him out the door.

When Sam and the kids met at his car in the hospital parking ramp, all of them got into the car without saying a word to each other. Only the sound of the car doors closing could be heard echoing through the ramp. Sam started the car, and then looked backward to pull out of the parking spot. When he turned his head, all of the kids were staring at him in awe. On the way to school, no one said a word to one another. They all understood what had happened. Nothing needed to be said.

Chapter 30

Sam and the kids pulled into the parking lot of Cayuga just before the morning buses arrived. Sam told each of them to keep the events of the morning secret, because any information that leaked out could prove to be detrimental to either Paige or themselves. If anything did get out, and they were questioned about it, he told them to allow him to take responsibility for all that happened at the hospital. He would say that it was all his idea and that the kids were merely doing what they thought was best for their friend.

As soon as Sam walked into school, he walked directly to the main office and told Mrs. Gillette that he had to see Mr. Massina immediately. She explained that he would be attending meetings all morning at district office and would not be able to see him until later in the day. Sam had intended on seeing Massina yesterday to discuss Paige, but never had the chance to because he had raced out of the building to go the hospital. He wanted to notify Massina as soon as he had contacted CPS because he did not want his administrator, who had up to this point treated him so decently, to be caught unawares by the news.

As Sam walked down C-Wing to his classroom, he began to feel extremely light-headed and became so nauseous and dizzy that he had to stop midway down the hall and lean up against a locker. When he finally made it into his room, he collapsed in his chair. He knew what was about to come; he always suffered physically after he performed a healing. Only this time, the symptoms were more severe. As the day wore on, Sam's physical state began to progressively deteriorate. By 8th period, he was not only feeling faint and nauseous, but he was also experiencing stabbing pains in his hands, feet, and side. To Sam it felt as though hot irons were being pierce into his body. Strangely, every bone in his feet and hands felt like they had been broken.

When his 8ᵗʰ period students finally arrived, the first thing they noticed was that he was not at his door to meet them. When Andrew, Daequan, and Olivia walked in they intended on acting nonchalantly about what had occurred earlier in the day, but the sight of their teacher shocked them. This was not the same man they left several hours ago. Sam was ghostly pale and sweating profusely through his shirt. When he slowly walked out from behind his desk and up to the front of the room, it looked as though every step he took was excruciatingly painful. By this time, every student in the room knew something was wrong.

"Mr. Amonte, what's wrong?" asked Mason.

Concerned, Daequan walked up to the head of the room where Sam was seated, and placed his hand on his teacher's shoulder and whispered to him he was going to get the nurse. Sam told him that he was "okay" and instructed him to return to his seat and work on his essay. In fact, he softly announced to the entire class that they could have the rest of the class period to work on their essays. Most of the students started to work, but Daequan, Olivia, and Andrew just pretended to work as they kept a concerned eye on him.

Mrs. O'Brien, who had dropped off Andrew at the beginning of the period, returned to class and immediately noticed that Sam did not look well. She watched with concern as he struggled to walk over to Alexandra's desk to answer a question. Mrs. O'Brien looked at Andrew and asked him what was wrong with Mr. Amonte. Andrew said he did not know what was wrong, but whispered that he was worried about him.

As he stood over Alexandra's paper reviewing her conclusion, Alexandra stared at him with concern. While desperately trying to concentrate on her essay as he battled through the pain, Sam suddenly thought he heard the sound of water dripping upon newspaper. First, it was the sound of one drop, then there was another, then several more in rapid succession. When he looked down to see where the noise was coming from, he caught a glimpse of Alexandra and realized that she had a look of terror on her face.

What Sam had thought was the sound of water dripping was actually droplets of blood falling upon her essay lying upon her desk. For a moment, he was puzzled because he could not understand where the blood was coming from. He just stared at the blood-stained essay as the small pool of blood became ever larger. Then, suddenly it hit him—*he* was the source of the blood. The blood that had been pooling on Alexandra's paper was coming from his right hand. When he opened his hand and looked at it, he saw a gaping wound at the center of it.

Alexandra sprang out of her seat and screamed for Mrs. O'Brien. Mrs. O'Brien rushed over, saw the blood, and immediately called the nurse's office. She then ran back to Sam and spotted the wound on his right hand. She ran over to the sink and grabbed a large pile of paper towels, pressed it in his hand, and led him immediately out of the classroom to the nurse's office. Mrs. Wise met them halfway down the hallway and immediately started wrapping the wound with a cloth.

When they reached the nurse's office, Mrs. Wise had Sam lie down on a cot as she applied pressure to the wound; however, as soon as she got the bleeding of his right hand under control, she realized that he was now bleeding from his left hand as well. Upon seeing this new injury, she immediately instructed her aide to call an ambulance, and come over to help her attend to the second wound. As they both applied pressure to Sam's wounds, Sam drifted in and out of consciousness. When he finally regained consciousness, he felt a wet cold compress on his head and could hear the sound of an ambulance off in the distance. Mrs. Wise looked first to Sam, and then to Mrs. O'Brien and asked what had caused the injuries. Sam just shook his head, and Mrs. O'Brien just stood there speechless and in shock.

While still lying on his back, Sam looked up at Mrs. Wise and asked her why his feet were so wet. She looked towards him confused, and then slid down towards the foot of the bed to examine his feet. When she pulled off his right loafer, she realized that his black sock was indeed soaked. At that moment, she could not understand why it was so wet, but when she pulled off his sock, she saw something that rocked the thirty-year veteran nurse to the core—a wound eerily similar to the wounds on his hands. Mrs. Wise felt a rush of panic wash across her body as she walked over to her supply cabinet to get more bandages. When applying pressure to his foot wound, Mrs. Wise felt her legs grow weak causing her to go down to one knee. By the time the EMT's arrived, everyone in the nurse's office was reeling from what they had just witnessed.

Chapter 31

When Sam woke up, he was lying in a hospital bed at Highland Hospital. Just outside of his room, he could hear two hospital staff members having a conversation in low tones.

"Apparently, the school nurse asked him where the wounds came from and he indicated that he didn't know."

"Is there any indication that they were self-inflicted?"

"It's certainly a possibility due to the unusual locations of the wounds, but it seems unlikely. According to school officials, no one has reported or noticed any kind of erratic behavior. Although the wounds are quite deep, they're not consistent with a laceration; so they were not caused by a sharp blade of any kind. They also don't seem to have been caused by blunt force either because the x-ray results showed no broken bones in his hands, feet, or abdomen."

When Sam heard them say abdomen, he pulled back the bed sheet and lifted up his hospital gown, and saw a large bandage on the lower left-hand side of his rib cage.

"If they aren't self-inflicted, could someone else have done this to him?"

"Again, he did not indicate to school officials that he was attacked or harmed by anyone. He certainly did not arrive at school with the wounds. So, it's highly unlikely that he was assaulted at school."

"So do you think that he is telling the truth when he says he doesn't know where the wounds came from?"

"I simply don't know Jonathan. I was hoping you could find that out."

"Okay. Let me ask you one last question. Given what you know up to this point, can you medically determine the cause of his injuries?"

"Although I am still waiting for a few more test results, at this point in time, I cannot explain with absolute certainty what has caused these wounds. The wounds show a very unusual physiology, Jonathan. They look as though pressure emanated from the inside and tore through the muscle, tissue, and skin. Perhaps you can get him to open up to you and explain the cause."

"I'll see what I can find out. Can I go in now to perform my exam?"

"He is stable now. Go on in, he should be fine to answer some questions."

"Jonathan—one more thing … about his wounds …"

"Yes."

"I was on call when Mr. Amonte was admitted yesterday at 4:30 p.m. His wounds were quite severe at that time. I just finished examining his wounds a few minutes ago. The wounds I just examined are not sixteen hours old."

"I don't understand. You said that he didn't arrive at school with these wounds. How can they be older then?"

"Jonathan—I am not saying that they occurred earlier. What I am saying is that the wounds I just examined are what I would expect to see 7-10 days into recovery. Mr. Amonte's wounds are healing at a much-accelerated rate. While we may be lucky enough to find out the origin of these wounds, I don't know if I will be able to medically explain how his wounds have healed so quickly."

Dr. Jonathan Keith entered Sam's room puzzled and intrigued.

"Good Morning Mr. Amonte. My name is Dr. Keith. I am the hospital psychiatrist. How are you feeling this morning?"

"I'm feeling a lot better than yesterday, Doctor."

"So you remember what happened to you yesterday?"

"Pretty much so, doctor."

129

"I talked to Dr. Seabrook on the way in, and she said that your wounds were pretty severe when you were brought in by the ambulance. Do you recall how you sustained those injuries?"

Sam knew that he was going to have to be careful on how he responded to Dr. Keith's questions. He did not want to give him any cause to question his mental faculties.

"I had not been feeling very well yesterday and it got progressively worse as the day wore on. Then in my last period class, I looked down to find my hand bleeding. I think I blacked out in the nurse's office, and when I came to, I saw that my other hand and both feet were bleeding as well."

Dr. Keith continued, "Mr. Amonte has something like this ever happened to you before?"

"No sir." Sam replied.

"Mr. Amonte—did someone else cause those wounds on your hands and feet?"

"No doctor."

"Did *you* have anything to do with causing those wounds Mr. Amonte?"

"Doctor, I know what you are thinking—I did not purposely harm myself. I have no desire to cause myself physical pain."

As soon as Sam finished uttering his last response, he realized the psychiatrist would misinterpret its meaning.

"Mr. Amonte you said that you did not *purposely* harm yourself. Are you saying that you somehow *inadvertently* harmed yourself?"

"Dr. Keith, what I meant by that was, of course I have something to do with the wounds, it's my body, and it's happening to me. However, I do not know what has caused these injuries. Isn't that the job of the doctors?"

"Dr. Seabrooke is an excellent physician, and I am sure she will be able to get to the bottom of this."

Dr. Keith spent that next 20 minutes finishing his psychological examination of Sam. When he left Sam's room, he was met by Dr. Seabrooke.

"What do you think Jonathan? Were you able to find out anything?"

"Well, Mr. Amonte is clearly mentally competent. However, I did leave feeling that he was not been completely forthright with me. I am not saying that he was lying to me, but he was definitely not telling me everything. So, I guess it is up to you to explain what caused these injuries. "

Chapter 32

At 12:30 a.m. on Sam's last night in the hospital, he was awakened by a gentle touch upon his right hand. When he opened his eyes in the dimly lit room, he saw the elderly Hispanic orderly from yesterday on her knees at his bedside with his injured right hand clasped between her hands and her head resting gently upon it. When she realized that she had awakened him, she lifted up her head and looked into his eyes. With tears streaming down her face, she spoke in broken English, "Padre. Por favor, por favor ... ten misericordia. Mercy—please mercy. Ten misericordia."

Sam, still half-asleep, said, "What's wrong?"

"Mi nieta, está enferma. My granddaughter ... Anna ... she sick. Please help. Ayude a mi nieta. Por favor, por favor—ten compasión."

"Señora, what is your name?"

"Me llamo—Margarita Sánchez."

"Señora, why do you come to me?"

"I see you. You help little girl in ICU. Ella recuperó! She better! Not en la coma. No coma!"

"Señora, please. I'm sorry but—"

"No, please—tenga compasión, por favor compasión, Padre—Look, look!"

Margarita grabbed Sam's hands and showed him his bandaged palms.

Next, she went to the foot of the bed, pulled the covers back and touched his bandaged feet and said, "Look, see."

Then she moved away from the foot of the bed and touched the wound in his side.

While touching his side, she looked at him wide-eyed and said, "Estigma ... Estigma."

Sam looked at her puzzled. She knew he did not understand. She tried to think of the word in English, but could not think of it. Margarita suddenly pulled a rosary from her pocket and showed it to Sam. She pointed to Christ's hands, feet, and side on the rosary, and then pointed to his hands, feet, and side. Suddenly the word came to her, "Stigmata."

Sam looked at her with disbelief at first, and then became agitated.

"No Señora! No Jesus!"

Margarita looked at him imploringly, and reached into her uniform and pulled out a medal hanging from a necklace. She showed it to him and said, "Padre Pío—stigmata. He help. You help. Por favor, por favor."

Sam reached out, and pulled her hands away from the medal and said, "No Margarita!"

Margarita became even more desperate and starting searching through her pockets again. This time she pulled out a laminated prayer card with a picture of catholic saint on it—Padre Pio. She held the card up to Sam, and he turned his eyes away. She continued to plead with him.

"You save my Anna. You can save. Look—like Padre Pio. Por favor, por favor, Padre."

Sam tore the prayer card from her hand and shouted, "No!"

Margarita collapsed crying on the side of Sam's bed. The sight of her nearly reduced him to tears. While she sobbed at his bedside, Sam looked down at the prayer card that had dropped on his bed. He picked up the card and on it he saw an elderly man with short gray hair and beard with his gloved hands folded in prayer. As Sam stared at the picture, he realized that the man on the prayer card seemed familiar to him. Moreover, it was not that he had just seen a picture of him before—he felt as though he had actually met this man before.

Suddenly, Sam was startled by a voice coming from the dark corner of the room. The voice temporarily frightened him because he had not noticed the presence of another person in the room. The voice that spoke was soft and gentle, "Abuelita, no llores." "Don't cry Grandma. It's okay."

Out of the shadows came Margarita's young granddaughter Anna. Anna was dressed in a light blue hospital gown. Most of her hair had fallen out from the effects of a combination of radiation treatments and chemotherapy. Large dark circles outlined her eyes. As she bent over comforting her grandmother at the side of the bed, Sam slowly rose from his hospital bed and took Anna by the hand.

Within a few minutes, an intensely bright light bathed everyone in the hospital room.

Chapter 33

After healing Anna, Sam took a turn for the worse, and was forced to stay in the hospital for another three days. The day that Sam was released from the hospital, he rested on his bed at home staring at the ceiling thinking about what had occurred that night with Margarita and Anna. Until that night, he had never thought of his ability to heal as being religious in origin. Sam believed in God, but he never considered himself, or what he was able to do, as being connected to Jesus or some saint. For him, it was just a part of who he was, not something mystical in origin. However, seeing the image of the man on the prayer card, the saint, who Margarita called Padre Pio, made it difficult for him to dismiss outright the spiritual aspect of his gift.

The image of the man on the prayer card hung there in the darkness in front of him. He could not get it out of his mind. Unable to sleep, he decided to get up and search the internet for information about Padre Pio. His search immediately generated numerous sites on the Catholic saint. As he scrolled down the page, he searched for sites that seemed less religious and more secular in nature. He finally found a site that outlined just biographical information on Padre Pio.

According to the website, Padre Pio was born in 1887 in a small town located in southern Italy called Pietrelcina. As early as age ten, he knew he wanted to devote his life to the church and reported to have had conversations with Jesus, Mary, a guardian angel, and even suffered attacks by the devil. Growing up, Padre Pio thought these holy visits were normal and that everyone experienced the same. Suffering was a constant part of his life for he was afflicted with numerous debilitating illnesses. In the early 1900s, he joined the Capuchian Order and became a priest in 1910. Eight years later, his life changed drastically when he acquired the visible stigmata—the five wounds of Christ after having been visited by Jesus and Mary. He would bare these wounds on his hands, feet, and side for fifty years until just before his death in 1968. Even though he was embarrassed by the wounds and sought to keep them secret, the news of the stigmata eventually spread to the outside world. Once it was known outside the Order, people began accusing him of all sorts of things: insanity, having intercourse with women in the confessional, misusing church funds, and ultimately self-mutilation to gain fame. From the mid 20's to the early 30's, church leaders tried to distance themselves from him and denied that the stigmata was divine in nature, and even prevented him from saying public mass and hearing confessions. It wasn't until the mid 60's that the Church dismissed all accusations against him and embraced his sanctity.

As Sam read the information on the site, he tried to convince himself that there were no strong parallels between Padre Pio's life and his own. He had never experienced a religious calling. He had never thought of living his life as a priest. He laughed to himself, "Me a priest!" He didn't suffer from illnesses his whole life, and he certainly didn't have visions of Jesus or Mary. And when last he checked, he hadn't seen the devil—let alone battled with him.

Yet, he couldn't deny that Margarita clearly noticed something spiritual within him. During their encounter, there was not a hint of doubt in her eyes when she approached him to help her grandchild. The only thing that seemed to frighten her was the possibility that he would choose *not* to help. Margarita's faith was so strong that night that it was palpable. He felt it surging within her when she touched him. The faith that she held within her heart filled him with fright and envy at the same time. This was a feeling that had eluded him his whole life. He wanted to have an explanation for the events that had occurred in his life, but it never occurred to him until that night it could be divine in nature.

He could not deny the fact that there were some glaring similarities between Padre Pio and himself. He did experience wounds eerily similar to the stigmata. They weren't long lasting like Padre Pio's, but they did occur after healing Paige. All his life he felt physical side effects after a healing, but nothing of the magnitude that he experienced after healing Paige. Why now did it occur? What about the older man that usually appeared during his healings? Like Padre Pio, he just accepted it as being normal. This old man who appeared from time to time was just a part of who he was. He didn't question his presence. However, that changed when he saw the picture on the prayer card. Could that person be Padre Pio himself? Certainly millions of Catholics around the world would believe it possible.

It wasn't until he read the information in the fourth website that he realized the most important parallel between Padre Pio and himself—Padre Pio's ability to heal. It was this similarity that had intensely drawn Margarita to his bedside that night.

The fourth website contained one account after another of the healing powers of Padre Pio. The first involved a woman who was given four months to live after being diagnosed with breast cancer. Her son-in-law asked Padre Pio for help during a confession. Padre Pio told him, *"We have to pray, everyone has to pray. She will recover!"* The woman recovered and went on to live nineteen more years. The next involved a 62 year-old man, who had broken both legs in a carriage accident and was told by doctors that he would never walk again without the assistance of two canes. During a confession with Padre Pio, Padre Pio told the man to *"Stand up and go away! You have to throw away those canes."* The man left the confessional and walked out of the church on his own. Next, a fourteen-year old boy with a deformed back was cured by Padre Pio after laying his hands upon him after confession. Yet another involved a thirty-eight year-old woman with intestinal cancer who visited Padre Pio before her surgery. When the physician opened her up on the operating table, he discovered that the cancer had disappeared. The doctor himself called it a miracle. The incidences of healing during his life and after his death were well documented and numerous.

Sam sat there and wondered what Padre Pio felt after he healed others. Was it the same way that he felt after saving Jimmy? Paige? He wished that the old man who came to him on these occasions would reveal himself to him, speak to him, and explain the mystery of it all.

Chapter 34

On Sam's first day back to school after being hospitalized, Mr. Massina greeted him in the main office.

"Mr. Amonte, I am going to need to see you in my office immediately."

"Yes Mr. Massina. I was just coming in to …" Mr. Massina turned his back to Sam and said to his secretary, "Mrs. Gillette, I want you to find an aide to cover Mr. Amonte's first period class while he is in a meeting with me."

"Mr. Massina—I can explain …"

Mr. Massina turned back towards him and said, "Mr. Amonte, I want you to go and get one of your union representatives and meet with me in my office as soon as possible."

"Please Mr. Massina; I don't need a union representative to talk to you."

"Listen, Sam—do *not* come to my office without a union representative. Disciplinary action may occur as a result of this meeting. Do you understand?"

Massina turned to Mrs. Gillette and said, "As soon as Mr. Amonte selects a representative to meet with him, please provide class coverage for that individual as well."

With that last statement, Massina retreated to his office without further comment.

Mrs. Gillette could barely look Sam in the eye. He could see in her eyes that she had heard this type of conversation before in her career, and it was not good.

"Sam, do you know what union representative you will have in the meeting with you?" said Mrs. Gillette.

"Ms. Petrucci—I guess."

"I will arrange coverage for her immediately."

Sam left the main office and walked down the front hallway with his heart pounding. Even though he anticipated that something like this would occur, the seriousness and formality in both Massina's voice and manner threw him off-balance. He had taught long enough to know that when an administrator instructed you to get a union representative, your job could be on the line—especially a teacher who was non-tenured.

When he arrived at Angelina's classroom, Angelina shot up from behind her desk and ran over to him with a look of great concern on her face.

"Sam, what's wrong? Are you okay? Why haven't you returned my calls? I have been worried sick about you."

"I'm fine Angelina. Don't worry—I'm good. However, I just walked in and Massina wants to see me in his office with a union representative. Can you come in with me?

"Why Sam? What's wrong? Is this about Paige?"

"It has to be." he replied.

"Listen, I have been doing some more research and talked to a few of our union leaders as well," said Angelina. "You cannot get into trouble for contacting Child Protection Services. The school district is prohibited from seeking any kind of disciplinary action against you for filing a report with CPS. This is wrong, and I will make sure that Massina knows this."

"Angelina, that's good news, but I am not too sure it is as simple as that. I haven't talked to you for a few days … some other things have occurred with Paige since we last talked.

"What do you mean? What has happened?

"Angelina … I cannot begin to explain to you right here and right now all that has occurred over the past few days."

"But Sam, I need to know everything before I go into that meeting. How can I protect you if I don't know all the circumstances of the situation? Please you need to tell me."

"Listen Angelina, I know we haven't known each other for a long period of time, but I care very deeply for you—this conversation cannot occur at this time and in this place. Just trust me for now."

"Okay. But listen—if things start to get out of hand in there and I feel uncomfortable with what is going on, I am going to call an end to the meeting, and ask the union leadership to come over and represent you."

"That sounds fine Angelina. I am so sorry to have to get you involved in this, but you are the only one I trust."

At that point, Angelina's phone rang—it was Mrs. Gillette informing them that Mr. Massina was waiting in his office.

When Sam and Angelina walked into Massina's office, Vice-Principal Cochran was at the conference table next to Massina. Massina instructed them to both sit down and informed them that Mr. Cochran would be taking notes during the meeting. Angelina echoed that she would be doing the same.

Massina did not waste any time starting the meeting.

"Sam did you contact CPS regarding Paige Lohrman?"

"Yes, I did." replied Sam.

"Did you not feel that this incident was serious enough to share the details with me?"

"Mr. Massina, I was not trying to hide this from you in any way. I trust you fully and respect you."

"Then why didn't you report this serious matter to me?"

"Sir, I did attempt to talk with you about this. My intent was to meet with you at the end of the day when I left early. However, when I heard Paige was in a coma, I was so concerned that I felt I had to get to the hospital immediately. The next morning, I spoke to Mrs. Gillette as soon as I arrived at school, but she said that you were in meetings for the remainder of the day. As you know, that was the day that I was taken to the hospital."

Mr. Massina seemed to be momentarily placated by Sam's response; yet he continued his questioning.

"Did you consult with anyone before filing this incident with CPS?"

"Yes, I did. I spoke at length with Mr. Corwin about the matter."

"And how did he respond to your concerns?"

Sam looked down for a moment and said, "He did not agree with my assessment of the situation."

"So despite his 30-plus years of experience in education, you decided to ignore him?"

At this point, Angelina interrupted, "Mr. Massina, you said that this matter could result in disciplinary action. Are you seeking disciplinary action because Sam filed a CPS report? Because if you are ..."

Massina interrupted Angelina immediately. "Angelina, you've known me a long time, have I ever violated the union contract or done *anything* improper regarding the administration of this building?" Massina paused and Angelina shook her head indicating that he had not. "So please do not attempt to inform me of the law; I am well aware that I cannot seek disciplinary action for a teacher filing a CPS report."

"Then what is this all about?" asked Angelina.

Massina opened up a file folder and leaned forward towards Sam.

"Let's forget the fact that you left the building without my permission for the moment. When you left the building, did you go to Highland Hospital to see Paige?"

"Yes, I did sir—I was concerned about her well-being."

"Did you speak to Mr. Lohrman while you were there?"

"Yes."

"Did you at any point in the conversation, place your hands upon Mr. Lohrman?"

"Yes, I did."

Angelina had not anticipated the direction that this meeting was now taking and started to get uncomfortable.

"Did you pin him up against the wall?"

"Yes."

"So are you admitting to me that you assaulted him?"

Angelina immediately stood up and said that she no longer felt comfortable in this meeting and advised Sam to end the meeting until the union president could step in to represent him. Sam told Angelina that he did not need any other representation and had nothing to hide from Mr. Massina.

He responded to Massina's question, "Sir, Mr. Lohrman came at me first. I simply defended myself. I, in no way harmed him. I simply took a hold of him to stop him from assaulting me."

"That is not what Mrs. Lohrman claims. She contacted the Superintendent of Schools and claimed that you came into Paige's hospital room making wild accusations about harming her daughter and then assaulted her husband. She is talking about filing charges with the police."

"Her statement is only partially true, sir. I did go there to warn Mr. Lohrman that his wife was poisoning his daughter. However, I did not assault Mr. Lohrman."

Mr. Cochran wrote the exchange down on his legal pad.

"Sam, I will come back to this issue in a few moments. Did you return to the hospital the next day even though you were warned by the family not to return?"

"Yes, Mr. Massina."

"Did you return with students as well?"

"Yes."

"Did you receive permission from their parents to transport these students in your own vehicle?"

"No, I did not sir."

"Do you know that it is against district policy to transport students in your personal vehicle without parental permission?"

"No, I did not."

"Okay," said Massina. "Did you enter Paige's hospital room on that day?

"Yes."

"What did you do when you were in her room?"

Sam knew how terrible his next words were going to sound to everyone in the room.

143

"I talked to her and touched her sir."

Angelina, visibly shaken, struggled to transcribe as her hand trembled.

"Where did you touch her Sam?" said Massina. Mr. Cochran looked up from his notepad at Sam as he answered.

"I touched her face, Mr. Massina."

"Did you touch her anywhere else Sam?"

"I did not, Mr. Massina! I swear to you!"

"Sam, the Lohrmans are accusing you of possibly doing something improper to Paige. They feel you cooked up this elaborate scheme because you are obsessed with her. Do you understand what they are accusing you of?"

"Mr. Massina—look at me. I did *not* touch Paige inappropriately. I am not obsessed with her in some inappropriate way."

"Then why did you go to her hospital room on that day? Why did you feel the need to use students to go and see her? Why did you touch her?"

Sam looked down as he wrung his hands on the top of the table. Fifteen seconds went by, and Sam had still not answered the question.

Angelina could not believe that this was happening. She wondered if she had completely misjudged his character.

Mr. Massina spoke again, "Sam would you like me to repeat the last question?"

"No sir."

"Well?"

"I went there on that day to save her."

"What do you mean—*save her*", Massina said in a stern tone. "She is in the best hospital in the city and being treated by one of the most prominent physicians in the state. What could you do that they couldn't?"

"Save her life."

"What are you talking about? I don't understand—she's in a *hospital* dammit!"

144

"Sir … I tried to tell them what was wrong with her. I told Mr. Lohrman about the Coumadin injections his wife was giving to Paige. Why do you think she was in a coma? Mrs. Lohrman had pumped her up with so much of it that it caused a brain hemorrhage. I told Mr. Lohrman to tell the doctors—he wouldn't listen. This young girl was dying, and I couldn't wait to see if they were going to figure out what it was. She was going to die! I couldn't let that happen!"

At this point, Angelina could no longer keep out of the conversation.

"Sam, I don't understand. How did you save her? The damage had already been done. What could you have done to save her?"

Instead of looking down feeling ashamed and embarrassed like he has his whole life, Sam sat up straight in his chair and said, "Because Angelina—I have the power to heal."

As the room fell silent, Sam scanned each of the faces before him. Cochran had a look of disgust on his face. Massina had a very different expression; it was neither anger nor contempt, it was one of disappointment and pity. The look a father would give when discovering their child had done something wrong.

Sam was afraid to look at Angelina's face. Other than his family, there was no one in his life that he cared more about than her. She was the last person he wanted to disappoint, or hurt. When he shifted his eyes from Massina to her, he only saw the top of her head as she stared at her notepad. His worst fear played out in front of him—she could not even look at him.

Mr. Massina closed his folder and instructed Cochran to immediately stop documenting the conversation. He looked to Sam and said, "Sam, listen to me. Are you sure you want that last statement placed in the record? Do you want to take another minute to respond?"

145

Sam never did respond to Mr. Massina's question. He didn't have to. Angelina responded for him. "You heard him Mr. Massina—he saved Paige's life."

Chapter 35

"Mr. Massina, Superintendent Whittig will see you now."

Mr. Massina had been called to Dr. Whittig's office to discuss the upcoming school board meeting regarding Sam's employment in the district. Dr. Whittig had been working hard over the past week to diffuse the situation and keep it out of the press. Throughout that time, the Lohrmans had been pressing him hard to have Sam terminated immediately. They portrayed him as dangerous and unfit to be in the presence of children. The teacher's union on the other hand, was trying to convince him that Sam was a credit to the profession. He had risked his job, and possibly his career, to ensure the safety of a child. As for the school board, they were divided. Due to the influence of Mr. Lohrman on the Board, he had easily convinced some members that Sam was a menace. Others preferred to hear all the facts first before making a decision.

Dr. Whittig always relied heavily on the judgment of his building principals to help him make recommendations on the retention of teachers, so he wanted to hear firsthand from Mr. Massina his assessment of the situation.

"Charlie thanks for coming in to see me. I appreciate all you have done to keep me informed and apprised of the situation at your building." said Dr. Whittig.

"You're welcome. It has been a tough year at school with Jim Merriman dying, and then this. It has been the most difficult year of my career."

"And you have done an excellent job. I'm sorry all this has happened in your building, but at the same time, I'm glad I have my best administrator handling it."

"Thank you, Dr. Whittig."

"Charlie, I asked you here because I have to make a recommendation to the school board regarding Amonte's future employment, and whether or not to file 3020A charges against him. The Lohrmans want the charges filed and have his teaching license taken away. I wanted to hear from you one last time before I make my final recommendation. I'll be honest with you Charlie; right now I think the best thing to do is terminate his employment and file the 3020A charges. This has the potential to become a bigger mess. So far, we have been able to keep this out of the press, but I don't know how much longer it will stay that way. The Lohrmans are respected members of the community and have a lot of influence, and they already have some board members calling for his head. Due to the fact that he is a non-tenured teacher, it might be best to just let him go. I might be able to convince the board to allow him to resign rather than terminate him. This could at least allow him to continue teaching, but I will not even consider that without your recommendation."

"Dr. Whittig I totally understand your position. If I were superintendent, I would want to end this quickly and quietly."

"Charlie, I sense some reluctance on your part. Listen, I didn't call you here to agree with me—I want you to be open and give me your honest opinion."

"Then I am going to come right out and say this to you sir; Sam Amonte should *not* be fired. In fact, I would consider myself fortunate to have him as a part of my staff."

Dr. Whittig could tell from previous reports and conversations that Massina seemed to have an affinity towards Sam, but he had not expected him to come out with such an unequivocal statement.

"Charlie, do you understand what you are asking me to do?"

"Sir, I am not asking you to do anything. I am just telling you how I feel as a principal. I know that in today's society that this is no longer *en vogue*, but I will never forget the Latin phrase that was drilled in my head by one of my education professors—*in loco parentis*—in *place of the parents*. I never understood the magnitude of my responsibilities as an educator until I heard this phrase. When our students are with us, we as educators, assume all rights, duties, and obligations of a parent. They are our children when they are with us. I have never forgotten the weight of that phrase. Therefore, every time I evaluate a teacher I ask myself, *"Would I trust this person to assume my responsibilities as a parent when my child is with them?"* If I cannot comfortably answer, *"Yes"* to this question, then I do not want that person teaching in my building. Dr. Whittig … I would want my children to be taught by Sam Amonte."

Massina continued, "I spoke at length with him about the situation. He made the right decision going to CPS. Based upon his account of the situation, he had every right to believe Paige was in danger. As a matter of fact, if he ignored the situation and did not act upon it, I would have made sure he never taught in my building again."

"Okay, put the CPS question aside for a moment—"said Dr. Whittig. "But Charlie—going to the hospital with children, getting into a physical confrontation with the school board president, accusing the wife of a school board member of poisoning her own child, sneaking into the hospital room? How is that supposed to be explained to the board and the community?"

"I know that it does not look good, or sound good. It is very easy to portray his behavior as extreme, or unstable. However, this young man risked his career for a child. How many teachers have you come across in your career that have been willing to do that? Mr. Lohrman may not realize this now, but Amonte may have saved his daughter's life. This is a man you want teaching *your* children Dr. Whittig."

"I'll do what I can Charlie, but I can't make any promises. I appreciate your honesty and candor."

As Massina walked out of the office, Whittig's last statement weighed heavily upon him. He was not totally honest with Whittig. He didn't share with him everything he knew. In his report and in his conversation, he did not share the fact that Sam stated he had the power to heal. He knew that a statement such as that would have sealed Sam's fate.

Chapter 36

A telephone rang in the *Times Union* newspaper offices and staff writer Paul Spence answered the phone, "Paul Spence."

The person on the other end of the line spoke, "Uhh, yes, Mr. Spence, I was wondering if I could talk to you about an important matter."

"May I ask to whom I am speaking?" said Spence.

"Well ... Mr. Spence, I really do not want to identify myself. I do not want to jeopardize my job. So, I would rather not at this point."

"Okay sir—what can I do for you?"

"I wanted to make you aware of a situation occurring in the Cayuga school district. As a member of our school community, I am appalled at what is occurring."

"How do you feel notifying me will help in this situation, sir?"

"I was hoping Mr. Spence, that if you made the community aware of the situation, then it will force the school district to do the right thing—to do what's right for the children of our district."

"Can you be more specific sir? Does this involve school district policy, an incident involving students, a personnel matter?"

"All of those, but most importantly—the conduct of a teacher."

"Did this teacher commit a crime?" said Spence.

"Possibly, but it is much more involved than that, Mr. Spence."

"Why don't you start from the beginning, sir?"

Two days later, Angelina showed up at Sam's apartment at 6:00 a.m., several hours before the start of school. When he opened the door and saw her face, he could instantly tell that something was wrong. In her hand was a copy of the *Times Union*, and she showed him a headline on the front page:

150

Substitute or Savior? Sam took the paper from her hand and placed it down on a small foyer table. Sam knew that it was only a matter of time before this came out in the open. He then reached out to her and pulled her close.

"Don't worry—" he said, "everything will be okay."

Across town, Dr. Whittig sat down at his desk in the district offices as his assistant brought in his morning cup of coffee and the newspaper. As he raised the hot coffee to his lips, he glanced down at the headline and spilled coffee into his lap. As he rose in his chair cursing and wiping his pants, his assistant came running in to see what was wrong. He growled,

"Get me Massina on the phone immediately and contact the school board—I need to see them in my office at nine o'clock sharp!"

A mile away, Mr. Massina was walking into the main office of Cayuga High, and he could tell after 15 years of working with Mrs. Gillette that the news that she was about to give was not good. She looked at him and said, "You haven't read the newspaper yet have you?"

"No, I haven't. Why?" he replied.

She did not even want to attempt to explain, she just showed him the headline. As he walked into his office reading the article, the telephone rang and she announced to him that Dr. Whittig was on the phone.

Meanwhile, in the Lohrman home, Mr. and Mrs. Lohrman, along with a very healthy looking Paige, sat at the breakfast table. Mr. Lohrman sat silently reading the newspaper, until he abruptly slammed the newspaper on the table. Paige and her mother looked up from their plates startled. Mr. Lohrman picked up the newspaper and told Mrs. Lohrman to follow him to the bedroom.

When she entered the bedroom Mr. Lohrman closed the door and said, "Wendy, please tell me that you had nothing to do with this?"

Mrs. Lohrman looked at him puzzled, "What are you talking about, Alec?"

He thrust the paper in front of her. She grabbed the paper and quickly began reading the article. As she read the article, her demeanor gradually changed. With each passing sentence she read, she became less startled and seemingly satisfied.

In a very cold and detached voice, she said to her husband, "I had absolutely nothing to do with this Alec, but I wish I did. It is about time someone found out about him. I have waited too long for Whittig and the district to act upon this. So they temporarily suspended him—big deal. He could end up back in the damn classroom for God's sake. This man is sick."

"Wendy, you don't get it. Do you understand what this is going to do to our daughter? The press isn't going to stop here. It will only be a matter of time before they find out our daughter is involved—if they don't know already! They are going to milk this story for all it is worth. His side of the story is going to come out eventually and when it does …"

"And so what if it does?" Mrs. Lohrman shouted. "You sound like you are defending him. He said that *I* was poisoning our daughter. I have devoted my entire life to protecting Paige from harm. I have given up almost everything in my life for her."

Mrs. Lohrman became more enraged with each word she uttered.

"You haven't been the one who has taken her to the countless doctors' appointments, exams, scans, procedures. You aren't the one that has had to administer treatments to her every day. I am the one who has sacrificed everything for our daughter."

"That is not fair, Wendy." Mr. Lohrman bellowed. "I have offered repeatedly to help you out. Every time I have attempted to take an active role in her medical condition, you have shut me out. It's always, 'You don't understand. You don't have the medical knowledge.' Well, I love and care for her as much as you do! I am not defending him. I just don't want our daughter's name dragged through the papers. She has been through enough."

Mr. Lohrman continued, "Did you read the entire article? This *Times* writer isn't coming out and saying unequivocally that

Amonte's a psycho and shouldn't be in the classroom. He's leaving the door open for people to interpret him as some kind of hero. Look at the damn headline—*Substitute or Savior?*"

"Look at this line Alec," said Mrs. Lohrman as she pointed to the newspaper.

"According to a source within the Cayuga School District, Amonte was quoted as saying that 'he has the ability to heal'".

"Anyone who reads this article is going to think he is nuts. A healer! Come on Alec."

Mr. Lohrman interjected, "I understand that Wendy. Yes, the vast majority are going to think him mentally ill. But there are also going to be a small number that are going to say that he was just doing his job contacting Child Protection Services. Then that is going to put the spotlight on our family—especially Paige. That is going to put us in the position of having to defend ourselves. I don't know what else this reporter knows. Obviously, someone is talking to him, and that person may not be done. We also don't know what Amonte may say to the newspaper either. It won't matter whether or not it is a lie—we end up getting dragged through the mud too."

He moved away from her, walked over to the bedroom window, and stared out into the street where Paige was standing with her friends.

Mrs. Lohrman walked over to him and in a calm and sympathetic tone said, "Alec ... Amonte can say anything he wants. He can say I was poisoning her with arsenic, Coumadin, whatever, but in the end, he is the one who is going to be seen as psychotic."

Mr. Lohrman immediately felt weak in the knees when he heard her say that word. He had never mentioned to his wife specifically what substance Sam accused her of poisoning Paige with during their confrontation at the hospital. Yet the word came out of her own mouth—*Coumadin*.

Mrs. Lohrman moved closer, hugged him from behind, placed her head on his shoulders and said, "Don't worry Alec, we are loved and respected in this community—people will stand by us."

Mr. Lohrman just continued to stare out the window and softly said, "Yes, dear."

Chapter 37

Sam and Angelina were lying together on his couch the night before the school board was to meet to decide his fate as a teacher in the district. He was on his back staring up at the ceiling and she was curled up beside him on her side with her hand draped across his stomach. For nearly an hour they sat there silent; yet it was not an awkward silence. With every stroke of his face, arm, and hands she communicated to him everything that he needed to know; he had found someone special.

Her words from the meeting with Massina the other day kept replaying in his mind—*"You heard him Mr. Massina—he saved her life."* He would not have blamed her if she walked out of the meeting and told him she never wanted to see him again. However, she showed an extraordinary faith in who he was; a faith that only his mother and grandmother had showed in him.

Sam knew that she must have had so many questions. Yet, she did not ask them. She knew that when he was ready he would tell her.

As he turned his head to look at her beautiful face, he decided it was time.

"It took me a long time to figure out the depth and breadth of this power. When I was young, I just kind of felt it was normal. It was who I was, and I didn't question it very much. It wasn't until I saw my father's reaction to it that I realized I was different. Unfortunately, my father made it very clear to me that this difference was something that he disliked in me. I mean, I loved my father and just wanted him to accept me and love me back; so I just spent a good part of my life trying to push it aside and bury it. This worked for a while, but ultimately that became just as alienating. I was living my life burying a huge part of who I was. If it wasn't for my mother, I don't know how I would have gotten through all this; her unconditional love has helped to sustain me all these years."

Angelina rolled over on to her stomach and propped herself up on her elbows to look him in the face and asked him when he last saw his parents.

"I left home when I was 18. That was the last time I saw them. I write to my mom as often as I can just to let her know I am okay. I tried to keep in contact with my grandmother as well, but I haven't heard from her in a while; she has been struggling with Parkinson's. She was such and positive and vibrant women; it hurts me not to be able to be with her and help her.

"You must miss them terribly. Haven't you ever wanted to go back and see them? I can't imagine not seeing my parents for so long," said Angelina.

"Angie, you can't imagine not seeing them because you love them so much. But that is the very same reason why I left. Both my parents had tough lives growing up—especially my father. All throughout my childhood, my mother always told me how blessed she was to have met my father and fell in love. Even though my father never communicated that to me, my grandmother always told me how their marriage changed my father for the better. She felt his love for my mother saved him. I saw what my gift was doing to them; it was driving a wedge between them. I couldn't do anything to jeopardize that love."

Sam continued, "Listen; there is not a day that goes by that I don't think about getting in the car and showing up on their doorstep. I've telephoned their house on several occasions wanting to talk, but each time I just put down the phone. It has just been so long …They are getting so much older … So much time has passed … I just don't know …"

As his voice started trailing off, she could tell that he was upset and conflicted. She felt bad for bringing up the situation especially the night before the board of education meeting and wanted to say something to ease his mind.

"Sam, you can't change what has happened up to this point. What's done is done. You have to stop beating yourself up for leaving. What you did was an act of love. When you truly love someone you should be willing to sacrifice anything for them. You made the ultimate sacrifice for them. No one can ever question your love for your parents."

Angelina sat up and continued. "But think … your parents have been together for a very long time and from everything you have told me, their love is strong. Don't underestimate their love for one another and especially their love for you. A love between a husband and a wife is a special bond; however, it is no less special than a love between a parent and child. Look at yourself; you are the most wonderful, sincere, and genuine person I have ever met. A person like you does not subtract from people's lives nor diminish them; you bring only goodness and beauty. Don't deny them the love of their son any longer."

"I wish Jim were here to speak to you. I know what he would say to you. First, he would tell you once and for all to accept who you are—unconditionally. Secondly, he would say it was time to see your mom and dad.

Chapter 38

The morning of the board of education meeting, Mr. Massina was in his office reading the third installment in a series of articles about Sam by reporter Paul Spence. Since his first article was published, Spence had been able to obtain more detailed and specific information about the incident. He had clearly done his homework; someone or several people close to the situation were feeding him information. While he never specifically mentioned Paige's name in any article, it was clear to many around town that she was the subject of the articles.

Another thing that angered him about the articles was that Spence was no longer reporting in an unbiased manner. In his first article, he reported the facts that were available to him at the time with fairness and left the reader the opportunity to form their own personal judgments. However, as the story gained more notoriety, the articles turned more speculative and judgmental in nature. This morning's article contained very few new facts. Instead, Spence chose to publish only extreme views on the incident. The use of the term "savior" in his first article commanded the attention of many religious groups in the area. They were appalled at the idea that a person, especially a teacher, would consider himself a "savior" and purport to have the powers of Jesus Christ. Phrases such as "false prophet", "burn in hell", "corruption of young minds", "danger to the welfare of children" were used throughout the article. It was only at the end of the article, that he quoted an unidentified student who said that Sam was "the most caring and compassionate teacher he had ever had." The articles had turned this incident into something of a witch-hunt and Massina did not have much hope that Sam could come through all this with his job.

As he finished the article, Vice-Principal Cochran came into his office to discuss the suspension of a student. Cochran could tell that Massina's thoughts were elsewhere.

"Charlie, are you going to the board meeting tonight?" asked Cochran.

"Yes, I have been asked to be there by Whittig and the board. To tell you the truth, I don't want to be there at all. It is going to be a circus, and at the end of it all, an excellent teacher is going to be ruined. This whole thing just makes me sick."

Cochran looked at Massina with a puzzled look on his face and said, "Charlie, I know that you like him and all that, but do you seriously think this man should be in a classroom with kids?"

This comment had caught Massina by surprise. Up to this point, he had just assumed that Cochran had felt the same way as he did about Sam.

"Rich, I don't understand. You always had complimentary things to say about Sam. You observed him on several occasions and felt he was going to be an asset to Cayuga."

"Yes, I *did*. That's until I realized what a sick man he is." Cochran's face suddenly became contorted and red as his voice raised in volume.

"You always told me that you never wanted a teacher in your building that you wouldn't trust teaching your own kids. Well, I wouldn't let this son of a bitch near any of my kids."

"Rich, are you serious? He wouldn't hurt a fly. He's made amazing strides with these kids. You've seen him—he cares about children ..."

Cochran cut him off in mid-sentence. "With all due respect, wake up Charlie, this freakin' guy thinks he *is* Christ."

"He never said he was Christ! You were in the room Rich; at what point did he say he was Jesus Christ?"

"Listen Charlie, we have known each other for a few years, and I have learned a lot from you and have trusted you, but on this one—you are dead wrong. You simply don't understand the situation like I do, and can never understand it."

"What do you mean, '*I can't understand this situation?*' I've been a teacher and administrator for over 30 years. What do you have—seven years *total* in education?"

Cochran, who had been leaning over and resting his hands on Massina's desk throughout the confrontation, suddenly backed away from the desk and stood up straight and tall. In a soft, but confident voice he said, "I may not have more years in education than you, but I do know that I have more experience with the Lord Jesus Christ. And I can tell you without a shadow of a doubt the 3,000 members of my congregation disagree with you as well, and we are going to make sure he never teaches again."

It was at this point that Charlie Massina realized how Paul Spence had been able to gain access to all the information in his articles.

Chapter 39

At 6:55 p.m., the monthly session of the Cayuga Board of Education was finally called to order fifty-five minutes late. So many people were in attendance on this night that the school board was unable to reach a quorum because several board members were stuck in a traffic jam outside the district offices. Every local television station had cameras and reporters on the scene. As each board member arrived, reporters and camera crews scurried over to them to obtain a public statement on Sam's conduct as a teacher. Prior to the meeting, Whittig had advised each member to refrain from making any public statements before the actual board meeting and each wisely heeded his request.

In the boardroom itself, it was standing room only. At the front of the room behind a long curved table were the nine members of the Cayuga School Board and Dr. Whittig. In the front row of the audience were Massina, Cochran, and the attorney on retainer for the district, Thomas Kane. Beyond the front row, scattered throughout the audience were clusters of interest groups with various opinions of Sam: parents, students, teachers, reporters, and union representatives.

However, the most visible group to all on that night were the members of Cochran's church—The Truth. They held signs that said, "...*Many false prophets shall rise, and shall many deceive. Matt 24:11*", "*Beware of false prophets, which come to you in sheep's clothing. Matt 7:15*", "*Suffer little children to come unto me, and forbid them not: for such is the kingdom of God. Luke 18:16.*", and "*Teachers—Not False Prophets.*"

As president of the board, Alec Lohrman brought the meeting to order. After the minutes from the last meeting were approved, the agenda for the night's meeting was read. As soon as the audience realized the discussion of Sam's employment would take place in a closed session of the Board, people from the audience became angry and began to shout. Mr. Lohrman banged his gavel repeatedly upon the table until he was able to quiet the crowd long enough to speak.

"It has never been this board's policy to discuss personnel matters in public session. At 8:00, we will convene a closed session, and then resume the public session shortly thereafter to announce our decision. We are not sidestepping this issue, nor attempting to hide anything—this has always been our policy."

Just then, a parent from the audience shouted, "What about our input? Don't we have a say about who teaches our children?" Others quickly jumped in to shout the same sentiment.

Lohrman brought down his gavel once again and said, "All residents of this school district will be allowed to speak during the public expression portion of this meeting. If you wish to speak, please see the clerk and your name will be placed on the docket. However, we are only allowing 30 minutes for public expression." Immediately people began to rush over to the clerk to sign up.

Thirty minutes after the start of the meeting, Sam and Angelina arrived at district offices amidst a heavy thunderstorm. They were told by the Cayuga Teacher's Union President, Don Schultz to go directly to Meeting Room B and await the arrival of the superintendent and the school board. Sam and Angelina climbed out of the car, threw their coats over their heads to shield themselves from the rain, and made a run towards the building. Sam was initially relieved to see that throngs of people were not outside awaiting his arrival, but this sense of relief was quickly replaced by an unsettling feeling. As Sam ran towards the building, he had noticed a man watching them from a car in the parking lot. The man looked familiar to him, yet he could not get a clear look at him through the rain and fogged windows of the car. When he reached the foyer of the building and brushed off his wet coat, he looked back at the car through the glass door, but by this time the car was empty. As they walked in, they were immediately greeted by a secretary and could see down the long corridor a large crowd spilling into the hallway outside of the boardroom. After sitting in Meeting Room B for nearly 30 minutes, they started to hear the voices of the crowd begin to rise in volume. Angelina reached over and clutched Sam's hand.

"It is deeply disturbing to the citizens of this community—", said one elderly man, "that a man such as this was even allowed in the classroom in the first place. Does the school district do any type of background check before they hire individuals off the street to teach our children?"

Lohrman responded, "Sir, I can assure you that we go to great lengths to make sure we hire individuals with impeccable backgrounds. As a matter of fact, our hiring process is often cited as being a model for others in the state."

A woman in her mid-thirties stepped up to the microphone next.

"What bothers me most is the fact that I was not made aware of the accusations against this man until recently. I had to find out in the newspaper that a teacher was taking children off school grounds without parental permission, physically attacking a parent, falsely accusing parents of child abuse, possible self-mutilation—the list goes on. Yet, I did not receive one letter from the school that any of this was going on. We put our trust in you to keep our children safe, and we should have the right as parents to determine whether an environment is safe for our children. Can you explain why we were not informed of this?

Another member of the Board spoke up due to the fact that the question directly involved the Lohrman family.

"As a government entity, we are bound to follow laws governing teachers as outlined in Educational Law. We had to investigate the situation first before we could make any public statements. We couldn't violate the rights of this employee by taking action before an investigation was even conducted. We performed due diligence in this matter. Unfortunately, details of the matter were leaked to the press before we could conclude the investigation."

Cochran shifted uneasily in his seat.

As the next speaker, a woman in her late forties walked up to the microphone, a man in his late sixties slowly weaved through the crowd from the hallway into the boardroom wearing a jacket, jeans, work boots, and a baseball cap. He stopped just inside the door and listened intently to the speaker.

The woman at the microphone had a Bible in her hand and read the following passage: *"And the beast was taken, and with him the false prophet that wrought the signs in his sight, wherewith he deceived them that had received the mark of the beast and them that worshipped his image: they two were cast alive into the lake of fire that burneth with brimstone..."*

Lohrman immediately interrupted the woman and said, "Madam, we are a public institution, we cannot in any way promote any form of religion at these public meetings."

"That is exactly the problem with public education Mr. Lohrman!" the woman fired back vehemently. "The only focus in education now is the dissemination of facts, theories, and formulas. What about the dissemination and acquisition of values and morals? Where are the role models for this generation of youth? Why is the greatest role model of all, Jesus Christ, forbidden from being mentioned in this school district? For me, and many other members in our congregation, we have had to swallow this bitter pill all our lives, but what has taken place over these last few weeks is an abomination. We've become accustomed to the neglect of our children's souls in public education, but this man Amonte is poisoning the hearts and minds of our children with his so-called miracles. We demand that this man be dismissed immediately and the district see to that he never steps foot in the classroom again."

With this last statement the crowd erupted. Daequan, Olivia, Andrew, Mason, Alexandra and many other students and teachers who came to support Sam started shouting across the room at the speaker and her followers. Lohrman slammed the gavel to the table repeatedly, but it was useless, the crowd was out of control.

Members of the Board huddled together, and Lohrman shouted over the crowd that he was suspending the remainder of the public expression and going into closed session. As they adjourned to Meeting Room B, the members could still hear the shouts coming from the boardroom.

Chapter 40

Sam could tell as soon as the board entered the room that they were visibly shaken. Personally, he felt no ill will towards them. In fact, he felt sorry for them that they were in this situation. He knew that he had put them between a rock and a hard place. Yet with this sorrow, there was no remorse. He would never feel sorry for saving Paige's life. The fact that others could experience negative consequences from the incident was regrettable, but he would not change a thing that happened.

Soon after the Board arrived, Massina, Don Schultz, and Thomas Kane followed. Lohrman was the first to speak.

"Due to the obvious conflict of interest in this matter, I am going turn the meeting over to Vice-President Tichnor. In addition, I am also going to abstain from voting in this matter." Schultz thanked Lohrman for his discretion and professionalism.

Tichnor started the proceeding. "Mr. Amonte ... I am sure that Mr. Schultz has apprised you of your rights at this meeting and that you understand the seriousness of the allegations against you?

Sam nodded and replied that he did.

"At the conclusion of this meeting, we as a board will make one of the following recommendations: continue your employment in the district, ask for your resignation, terminate your employment, or file 3020A charges against you and seek the revocation of your teaching license. Mr. Schultz was provided with a copy of Dr. Whittig's investigation into the matter. Did you read this report?"

"Yes, I have Mr. Tichnor," Sam replied.

"Is there any portion of this report that you would like refute or comment on?"

"Mr. Tichnor, I appreciate not only the accuracy and thoroughness of this report, but also the impartial manner in which it was prepared. The facts presented in this report are accurate, and I do not refute them."

Tichnor looked over at Schultz for some reassurance that Sam knew what he was saying. Schultz nodded in recognition.

"Well then Mr. Amonte, is there *anything* that you would like to say before we make our decision?"

"Only this Mr. Tichnor ... I cannot fully explain the events that have occurred recently. I know that all of you here want very much to hear some type of explanation from me: some for curiosity's sake and others because they want me to provide some plausible explanation to save my career."

Sam looked over at Angelina and Mr. Massina. "Unfortunately, I have none to offer. I have come to accept that not all of life's experiences can be explained. With all the advances we are making in science and technology, we've become overconfident, almost arrogant. We think we can control everything, solve any problem, and explain our world with certainty. Thinking this way, helps us to feel safe and secure in our daily existence. So when we come across things that we cannot readily explain, we brush it aside as myth, illusion, or fabrication. The truth is what we don't know about this universe is incalculable. What we know is infinitesimal compared to what we have yet to discover."

"Yes, I do believe I saved Paige's life on that day, and I would do it all over again if faced with the same situation. I am a teacher and my first priority is and will always be the health and welfare of the children who sit before me. If that costs me my job or my livelihood, then so be it."

Tichnor looked over to Dr. Whittig and Attorney Kane and asked if they wish to speak. Both men declined the offer. Tichnor concluded the meeting. "Mr. Amonte, at this time we would like you and your union representatives to leave the room and we will announce our decision when we reconvene the public session."

Tichnor waited for them to leave the room and immediately called for a vote, "I really don't see at this time a need for a lengthy discussion on the matter. We have all read the report, discussed the matter privately, and I did not hear anything from Mr. Amonte today that changes anything we have read or discussed up to this point. Therefore, would someone like to place a motion on the floor regarding the matter?"

A member of the Board spoke up. "I make a motion to terminate Mr. Amonte's employment with the district."

"Discussion?" said Tichnor.

The room remained quiet.

"All those in favor say, "Aye"."

Eight members of the Board cast a vote in favor of the motion. The ninth member, Mr. Lohrman sat in his chair scribbling on a notepad.

"Okay, the motion has passed." said Tichnor. "Let's now move on to the next issue. Should we file 3020A charges against Amonte and seek the revocation of his teaching license?"

"I would like to make a motion to file 3020A charges." said another member of the school board.

"Discussion?" said Tichnor. "Mr. Kane, could you advise the board on this complex legal matter?"

"Well, after reviewing the incident I do not see any pedagogical incompetence on the part of Mr. Amonte that you could use to pursue 3020a charges. I have read his appraisal reports and based upon these reports, he was considered by his principal and vice-principal to be a highly professional and gifted teacher."

A board member interrupted, "Are you saying that we can't touch him because he was considered competent in the classroom? What about all the things that occurred *outside* of the classroom? Falsely accusing a parent of endangering the welfare of a child, transporting children off school grounds without permission, the improper touching of a student … Oh yeah, how about the fact that the guy is insane!"

"To answer your question—" Kane said calmly, "we can still bring charges against him for conduct that occurred off school grounds. However, we need to show that there is a connection between the off campus conduct and the performance of his duties."

Tichnor spoke next. "Can you establish a link between his off-campus conduct and the performance of his duties?"

Kane opened up his file on the incident and commented on each off the off campus incidences.

"On the matter of falsely accusing a parent of endangering the welfare of a child … I'm sorry, but we should not pursue this charge. There was reasonable cause for him to come to that conclusion. Please Mr. Lohrman, do not take this the wrong way, I am not saying that you endangered your child in any way. What I am saying is that according to the law, if a teacher reasonably believes a child's welfare is endangered, then the school district cannot pursue litigation."

"I understand", Mr. Lohrman said solemnly.

Kane continued. "Yes, the transportation of students is serious, but you have already exercised what would be considered the appropriate disciplinary action in this matter—he has been fired. In my opinion, trying to prove him mentally incompetent would be a waste of time. I obtained a copy of the Highland Hospital's psychological evaluation by Dr. Keith when Mr. Amonte was admitted recently and it mentions *nothing* about him being mentally incompetent."

One of the board members had become intensely frustrated and agitated by Kane's legal interpretations.

"What about the fact that he admitted to touching Alec's daughter? Are you telling me molesting a child is not grounds for taking away a pervert's teaching license! What the hell is wrong with this damn country today?"

Just then, Lohrman yelled, "Enough!" The entire room fell silent.

"This man didn't molest my child. I don't want to hear any more talk like that. As much as I want him out of this district and out of our lives for good, I can't sit here and listen to you accuse this man of being a child molester. I don't like what he did and how he went about it, but I do believe one thing—he tried to protect my daughter. I can't sit here and watch you guys destroy his livelihood for doing what he thought was right for a child he was teaching. Let's just get this guy out of our district and end the matter once and for all."

"But Alec—" said Tichnor, "we have to think about …"

"Just end it!" shouted Lohrman.

The board took their vote and returned to the public boardroom to announce their decision.

Chapter 41

"That's it?" yelled out Cochran. "He gets to keep his license?"

Massina grabbed Cochran's arm and tried to pull him back into his seat, but he and other members of his congregation continued to shout at the school board. No one in the crowd seemed to be pleased with the decision and each was voicing their opinion loudly. The only person in the room that seemed to have his composure was the man in the Carhart jacket and baseball cap. He just stood there silently watching the reaction of the crowd.

As the board members filed out of the room amidst the shouts, people began to pour into the hallways and out in front of the building in pursuit. Mr. Schultz walked into Meeting Room B and announced the decision to Sam and Angelina. Sam did not react to the news, but Angelina was upset; Sam would no longer be teaching in Cayuga. Sam comforted her and told her that it would be all right and thanked Mr. Schultz for his representation.

On the way out of the building, Sam and Angelina realized that it was a mistake to leave so soon. At the exit door, Mr. Lohrman was surrounded by 20-30 people. When Sam and Angelina turned to go in the other direction, an even larger number of people were coming out of the boardroom into the hallway. As soon as they saw him, they started shouting at him. Sam grabbed Angelina's hand and pulled her in the direction of the exit. As they passed by the exit, Mr. Lohrman and Sam's eyes met for a brief instant. In that instant, Sam simply nodded.

When they finally reached the outside of the building, nearly one hundred people were outside the entrance of the building including the media and several police cars. By the time he realized it was better to go back inside, the entrance to the building was blocked with people. Microphones were shoved into

171

his face, and reporters were asking him questions that he could not make out over the din. Angelina desperately grabbed on to his coat, but was pried away from him by the push of the crowd.

As soon as he spotted Sam, the man with the Carhart jacket, who was on the outer edge of the crowd, began forcefully pushing his way closer to Sam. Due to his great strength, he was able to get within several feet of Sam in less than a minute. When a camera operator was pushed aside and fell to the ground, a small opening developed in the crowd and Sam saw the man in the Carhart jacket standing before him. Sam immediately recognized his face, but before he could say a word, the man lunged towards him. Instantly, a bright flash appeared before Sam's eyes accompanied by a deafening noise.

Sam had been shot.

People who were close by began screaming and scattering in every direction. After a second shot was fired, Daequan came racing out of the crowd and tackled the gunman to the ground jarring the gun loose from his hand. The gunman struggled to get free, but several others hurried in to help Daequan. Within several seconds, a police officer was able to reach the scene and handcuff the gunman.

On the national news that night, the only clear footage of the actual shooting came from the camera operator who was knocked to the ground immediately before the shooting. The incident was taped almost entirely from an angle with the camera on its side. The first five seconds showed Sam struggling to make his way through the crowd. Suddenly, the man in the Carhart jacket appears from the left in the footage, lunges towards Sam, and then *passes* him towards a man holding a gun. The man in the Carhart grabbed the barrel of the gun and the gunman's arm just before the weapon was fired. The first shot fired hit Sam in the head, grazing his right temple. Sam immediately fell to the ground. While Sam was on the ground, the gunman aimed a second shot towards him, but the man in the Carhart wrestled himself between them, and pulled the gun towards his own body.

After a few seconds of struggle, the second shot went off hitting the man in the Carhart in the abdomen. Next, viewers could see Daequan come into the shot knocking the gunman and himself out of view from the camera. At this point in the footage, the camera operator was able to regain his footing and bring the camera upright again.

As the camera slowly panned in, viewers could see the man in the Carhart lying on his back on the ground with his shirt soaked with blood. The camera then turned its focus on Sam who by this time had managed to struggle to his knees with his face, head, and neck awash in blood. As the camera panned back out slowly, Sam crawled over to the man in the Carhart and cradled his head into his arms. Among the screams and shouts, you could hear Sam saying to him,

"No! No! It's okay. I'm here Dad. I'm here."

The aired footage of the shooting ended there, however, much more occurred at the scene. Sam kept telling his father repeatedly that he was going to make everything all right. Mr. Amonte, who was clutching his wound with his left hand, lifted up his head towards Sam's face and tried desperately to speak to him. For several moments, his lips moved, but no sounds came out. Then Mr. Amonte's face contorted as a wave of pain shot through his body. Sam told him not to talk, but his father desperately wanted to say something to him. Finally, he pulled Sam down to his lips and said, "I'm sorry son."

With those words, his hand fell from Sam's face leaving behind a trail of blood.

When two paramedic crews arrived on the scene, the first crew rushed quickly over to Mr. Amonte and proceeded to treat him and the other crew attempted to treat Sam, but he kept pushing them away so he could get to his father.

"Leave me alone!" he shouted. "I have to help my father!"

Sam pulled himself free and pushed the paramedic who was treating his father to the ground. From his backside, the paramedic shouted to a police officer on the scene to restrain

Sam. As the police officer and Sam struggled, another officer intervened to assist. As the two officers held him back, Mr. Amonte was put on a stretcher and placed inside an ambulance. As the ambulance rushed away with sirens blaring and lights flashing, Sam could be heard screaming, "Don't take him away—I can save him!"

Chapter 42

When Mr. Lohrman arrived home from the school board meeting that night, he could hear the television in the living room.

"According to witnesses, an unidentified man approached the teacher, Sam Amonte, and fired two shots. The first shot apparently grazed his right temple and the second struck another person who was later identified by police as the father of Amonte—Anthony Amonte. Anthony Amonte can be seen in this exclusive Channel 13 footage stepping in front of his son and wrestling with the shooter before collapsing to the ground from a gunshot wound to the abdomen."

As the reporter continued on with the story, Mr. Lohrman closed the front door and began walking up the stairs to his bedroom. Upon hearing the door slam shut, Mrs. Lohrman began calling out, "Alec? Alec is that you?"

He ignored her shouts and slowly continued walking up the stairs as if he had the weight of the world on his shoulders. When he reached his bedroom, he began undressing and could hear his wife charging up the stairs still shouting his name.

"Alec—why aren't you answering me? What the hell happened tonight? Are you okay?"

"I'm fine Wendy," he answered in a low monotone voice as he continued to undress.

Mrs. Lohrman stared at him in disbelief.

You're fine? That's all you have to say. There was a shooting tonight for God's sake!"

Mr. Lohrman did not respond and turned his back on her as he took off his watch and placed it on the dresser.

"Alec!" Mrs. Lohrman cried, "Why are you not talking to me? Why are you treating me this way? How can you just stand there in silence?"

Upon hearing these words, he turned to his wife and said, "You know Wendy … You're right. Why am I standing here silent? It's wrong for me to stand here with my mouth shut. As a matter of fact, I have been guilty of that for far too many years now."

"What are you talking about Alec? What is wrong with you?"

"What's wrong with me you ask Wendy?" he said angrily. "I've got a better question—what the hell is wrong with you! Are you happy with what happened tonight? Does it make you feel better that Amonte was almost killed tonight, and his father is probably bleeding to death in an emergency room right now?"

"That is unfair Alec—" she replied. "I would be the first to admit that I despise that man, but I never wanted to see him killed. Do you know how many gunshot victims I have seen in my life? Let me ask you something Alec …Have you ever had your hands inside the chest of a person who is bleeding to death from a gunshot or shrapnel wound? You have no idea the things I have experienced during my tours of duty. How dare you? I have spent my entire life caring for the sick and wounded—I get no satisfaction from the suffering of others. How dare you!"

"How dare I?" he fired back. "Is that what you said Wendy?"

Mr. Lohrman walked over to his wife's closet and started to reach for something on the top shelf.

"What are you doing Alec? You know I do not like you going through my things."

Mr. Lohrman ignored her and pulled something down from the top self—an old shoebox. Mrs. Lohrman immediately lunged at him in an attempt to pull the shoebox from his hands. As she grasped the box, Mr. Lohrman, in a fit of rage, grabbed her by the arm and pushed her with such force that she was sent flying several feet across the room onto the bed.

Mrs. Lohrman attempted to scramble to her feet, but once again he pushed her back down on the bed and told her not to get up again. She did not attempt to move and lay there silent. For the first time in her twenty-year marriage, she was frightened by her husband and what he could do next.

When Mr. Lohrman opened the shoebox, he pulled out a small pharmaceutical vile, pushed the vile into his wife's face and said, "You listen to me very carefully ..." he said in a soft, but stern voice, "If you value our family—our marriage at all, you tell me the truth ... Did you inject our daughter with this?"

Mr. Lohrman stared intensely into her eyes hoping for some indication that he was wrong. Mrs. Lohrman quickly smothered all hope as she looked away from her husband's stare with tears streaming down her face. Mr. Lohrman's body collapsed upon his wife's as the weight of the stark and unnerving reality pressed down upon him. Both cried as they lay there upon the bed.

After crying for several minutes, Mr. Lohrman suddenly stopped. He quickly jumped off the bed and started to slowly back away in horror. Mrs. Lohrman rose from a prone position to her knees on the bed and faced her husband.

"Alec? What? What is it?" she said lifting her arms towards him trying to bridge the space between them.

"No! Oh God, no!" he cried. "No Wendy!"

"Alec—what? What is wrong? Please, I am sorry—I am so sorry," she said as she climbed off the bed towards him.

"No, don't come near me." he shouted. "The baby ... our beautiful baby—Emily. Did you..."

"No Alec!" she cried out as she fell to her knees. "I did not hurt her Alec, I swear to you. Her death had nothing to do with me. Honey, it was SIDS ... it was SIDS. Please believe me."

Mr. Lohrman grabbed her by the wrists and lifted her up from her knees so they were face to face.

"How can I believe anything you say? You tell me the truth Wendy! Did you kill Emily?"

She did not look away from him this time. She looked him straight in the eyes begging him to believe her.

"Alec, I admit it; I am not going to lie to you anymore. I may have made Paige sick by treating her, but it was because no one was listening to me. These doctors were not taking her illnesses seriously. They kept saying there was nothing wrong. I needed them to take me seriously—I am a medical professional too, I know just as much as they do. They don't care for my daughter like I do."

He looked at her incredulously, "Wendy, you are sick. Do you hear yourself? You need help."

"Alec, I swear … I will … I swear." she replied. "I promise you I will get help. But you have to believe me; I did not hurt poor Emily. Her death crushed me. Her death changed me forever. A big part of who I was was buried forever with her in that tiny casket."

All of a sudden, the Lohrmans simultaneously stopped talking. Both felt the presence of another person in the room. When they looked to their left, Paige was standing at the door with tears in her eyes.

"Ma … Mamma … *you* did this to me? You made me sick?" she said.

Mrs. Lohrman rushed over to her desperately trying to embrace and comfort her while Paige struggled to pull away. Mrs. Lohrman fell to her knees and grabbed Paige around the waist.

"Honey, please I didn't mean to hurt you. I didn't mean for you to get so sick. Honey—my sweet girl—please…"

Paige stared down at her crying mother as her world turned upside down.

Paige, weakened by shock and anguish, collapsed onto her mother's back, grabbed her shirt, and buried her face in it. As she rocked back and forth crying, she angrily shouted,

"You are my mother! You are supposed to love me! You are supposed to love me! You … are … supposed … to … love … me!

Chapter 43

"Are you okay Hon?" Angelina said to Sam as he looked through boxes in his grandmother's attic.

"Yeah, I'm okay. It's just really hard to believe that she is gone. I can feel her everywhere in the house. Her house is almost completely unchanged from when I was growing up: the same furniture, carpeting, pictures, knick-knacks—except she is not here. It just seems surreal to me. We should be out in the garden talking and laughing together."

"Sam, I found a few more boxes and a trunk in the basement that I want you to carry up," Sam's mother called out as she walked up the attic stairs.

When she came to the top of the stairs, Angelina gave her a look of concern, and she immediately knew that he was upset over the recent death of his grandmother. She put down the boxes that were in her hand and knelt beside him.

"It's going to hurt for awhile, but that hurt will eventually be replaced with beautiful memories of her. Remember, she loved you very much. She asked about you all the time while you were gone. She wanted so much for you and your father to patch things up again."

Sam looked at her and said, "I guess I disappointed her, huh?"

"Disappoint her?" she said incredulously. "She understood why you left and admired you for that. Yes, it hurt for her to see you leave. But in the end, she realized why you left and looked upon it as an act of love."

"Did she suffer, Ma?"

"Honey, as bad as things were at the end, there were still glimpses of your grandmother there. Her vitality and optimism would shine through for brief periods, and she *never* forgot you. In her hospital bed, she would touch her hands to her heart and say, 'Sam is such a beautiful boy; he had the heart of my Paul.' She loved your grandfather more than life itself, and you reminded her of him. So, you tell me if she was disappointed in you."

With that comment, she kissed him on the cheek and went over to help Angelina pack some items away.

As he sat there looking through boxes, he could not believe that four months had passed since the shooting. As quickly as he was in the forefront of the news cycle, it seemed as though he never existed—not a single newspaper article or news story had appeared for nearly three months. For Sam and Angelina, it was a blessing. Finally, he felt at peace. He had spent so much of his life trying to keep ahead of his past, that it was comforting just to be able to enjoy the moment.

There was not a day that went by that Sam did not think about the events that transpired during his time at Cayuga. In the past, when he left a district, he would force it out of his mind and try never thinking of it again. With Cayuga, it was different. The children there changed his life forever. Even though he and Angelina had since moved out of town, he still kept in contact with Daequan, Alexandra, Mason, and Andrew on a regular basis. All of them missed him sorely, and he missed them too. Unfortunately, he had to remind them that it would be best to allow more time to pass before they could see each other. He reassured them though, that they could call, text, or email him anytime.

The person he heard most often from was Andrew. Andrew made it a point to send him an email every week. The last email from Andrew was the best news he had heard in months. Andrew had been keeping in close contact with Paige since Sam left town. According to Andrew, Paige was in the best health that he has seen her in since elementary school. She had been in school every day since the shooting and was even cheerleading again. Paige told Andrew the other day that she and her father had been spending more time together and had been closer than she could ever remember.

Andrew even noticed a change in her mother as well. The last time all of them were over to her house, her mother did not hover over them, check in on them, or interrupt to administer medication. The most important news he received from Andrew was regarding the medical care she was receiving. Paige's *father* was now coordinating her medical care. Mr. Lohrman found a doctor who was able to take Paige off most of her medications and suggested taking a more holistic approach. Paige was the happiest he had seen her in years. Every letter he sent to him ended with the same statement, "Paige says, 'Hi', and she can't wait to see you again."

Sam looked over at his mother and Angelina on the other side of the attic. They were talking and smiling together as they packed away boxes. They came across some old pictures of Sam when he was a baby and were laughing at his chubby cheeks. They both looked over at him, and simultaneously pursed their lips together and blew air into their cheeks. They both fell over laughing. Sam looked over to them and smiled. He was so happy that his mother and Angelina had become so close in such a short period.

As far as his relationship with Angelina, they had grown even closer since the shooting. Because their relationship had been forged in the heat of public controversy and turmoil, it did not give them much time to reflect upon what they had together. Their relationship up to that point was based on raw emotion, attraction, and passion. However, he wondered how they would feel towards each other once life calmed down for them. Would the intense feelings they felt for one another continue to exist? After three months of relative quiet, he had his answer.

Each day that passed brought him a new discovery about the depths of her personality and heart. The traits that originally attracted him to her—confidence, intelligence, strong will, grace, and humor were real and lasting. However, as he came to know her better, he also discovered a wonderful sweetness and vulnerability to her. These endearing qualities made him want to be with her and protect her forever. He could not imagine life without her, and she made it clear to him that she felt the same.

"Ma, I am going down to the basement to check out those boxes and that big trunk."

"Okay Honey—they are underneath the stairs. Drag out that trunk, and see what is in it. It looks pretty old."

Trying to pull out the trunk was much harder than Sam anticipated. The trunk was very old and heavy, and by the amount of dust and dirt on it, it must have been there for quite awhile. When he was finally able to drag it out in the open, he noticed that mice had chewed away holes in several parts of the trunk. When he unfastened the latches and opened it up, he did not quite know what he was going to find inside. The fact that nothing moved inside was a good sign. Taking up most of the space in the trunk was a yellowed and stained wedding dress and veil. He carefully lifted the fragile garments out of the trunk and laid them on the floor. At the bottom, was a pair of shoes, a blue handkerchief, an ornate cameo pin and a photo album. Sam picked up the album, sat down on the floor and opened it up in his lap. As he paged through the album, he saw many photographs of his grandmother and grandfather on their wedding day and what looked like their honeymoon. It was great to see these other photos of his grandparents because the only picture he had ever seen of his grandfather was the one his grandmother displayed in her living room from their wedding day. He particularly enjoyed seeing the candid shots of them on their honeymoon in Maine. The picture displayed in his grandmother's living room was very formal with neither of them smiling. However, in the album there were many shots of them posing in silly positions on the beaches, trails, restaurants and parks of Maine. It made Sam smile to see them so animated and happy together.

Page by page, over the next hour, he reveled in the intimate, funny, and touching poses of his grandparents. When he went to turn the last pages of the album, he realized that they were stuck together. As he carefully separated the pages, a photograph slid from the pages then down between his legs. He picked up the picture, and on the back was written "San Giovanni Rotondo, Italy".

When he turned over the picture, the photo was slightly out of focus and grainy, he could see that there were two men in the photo—one in a uniform, which appeared to be from World War II, and one in what looked like some sort of robe. Sam moved the picture from side to side trying to catch the best light to see who was in the photo. When he caught the light just right, he said, "This ... can't ... be?"

Sam ran over to the workbench with the picture and turned on the overhead fluorescent light to get a better look.

As Sam studied the picture in more detail under the light, he could see that the man in uniform was his grandfather. He thought to himself, "That is definitely Grandpa, just a little older than the wedding photos. But the other man, it just can't be!"

Sam raced up the basement stairs, through the house, and up to the attic to show the picture to Angelina and his mother. When he reached the attic, he said, "I found this picture in the trunk. This man with Grandpa—do you know who he is?

As his mother looked at the picture, footsteps could be heard coming up the attic stairs. As soon as the footsteps reached the top of stairs, Sam, Angelina, and Mrs. Amonte looked over to the man standing in the entrance to the attic. The man walked over to them, took the picture in his hand, and said to Sam, "Son—the man with Grandpa is Francesco Forgione—Padre Pio."

Chapter 44

"C'mon, Sweetie let's go finish packing up the basement." said Mrs. Amonte to Angelina. She knew that it was time for her husband and son to finally talk.

"Dad, I don't understand? Grandpa with Padre Pio?"

"Please son, let's sit down and talk."

Mr. Amonte dragged over a large trunk for them to sit on. Sam sat down confused and agitated, until suddenly he rose to his feet and lashed out at his father.

"Please tell me you haven't known about this all these years? When I told you about the old man who came to me and described him to you; you never said one word to me. You made me feel like I was crazy or lying. You *knew* who that old man was all the time didn't you?"

Mr. Amonte tried to grab Sam's hand to calm him and sit him back down, but he forcefully pulled away from his father.

"Don't touch me. Just tell me the damn truth!"

"Son, I swear to you, I did not know for sure that the person who came to you during the healings was Padre Pio. I had my suspicions, but I didn't know that for sure."

"I don't understand; why would you even suspect it was Padre Pio in the first place?" Sam shouted. "What do your father and Padre Pio have to do with the things that happened to me?"

Sam stood there in front of his father waiting for an answer, but his father could not even look up at him.

Still angry, Sam repeated the question, "Why would you think that Padre Pio would come to me during a healing?"

Mr. Amonte finally looked up at him and in a soft voice said, "Because your grandfather had the same ability to heal."

Sam just stood there in the middle of the attic stunned by this revelation. However, as the revelation began to sink in, his feelings of anger began to dissipate into a sense of relief. He had always wondered, "Why *me*? Why was *I* chosen to have this power?"

Finally, after all these years, it was clear to him now— he wasn't a freak. This power was passed down to him from another—his grandfather. Somehow, someway, through the blessings of God and perhaps the vast genetic code, he inherited this power.

Mr. Amonte continued, "Why do you think your grandmother always said, 'You have the same beautiful soul as your grandfather.'? Why do you think she always compared you to him? It wasn't that you looked like him, or laughed like him—it was because she recognized that you possessed the same special powers as he did."

In a pleading tone, Sam said, "Why couldn't you just tell me this when I was growing up? I felt like a freak after healing Jimmy! Do you realize what I have been through my whole life? Is that why you never wanted to talk about Grandpa and had so much anger towards him—because of his ability to heal? Is that why you acted so cold and disappointed in me? Don't you understand that I grew up feeling as though you hated me?"

Mr. Amonte responded, "Son, I will never be able to forgive myself for how I treated you. It is a regret that I will take to my grave. No matter what happens between us from here on, it will never take away the pain and regret that I feel inside for treating you that way. Someday, you will be a father, and you will realize that the most important and challenging aspect of your life will be raising children. You will have so much love for your children that you will be willing to do anything to protect them. What goes hand and hand with this is the desire to see your child have a better life than you did. When you saved Jimmy that day at the ball field, I saw your life taking a parallel path to mine. After all that had happened to me, I wasn't going to let it happen to you. I didn't want you to have to experience the life that I did. Unfortunately, in doing that, I drove you away and hurt you deeply. I made a terrible mistake son; a father should never ask anything more of his son than to be loved, honored, and respected by him. You gave those three precious gifts to me, and I should have accepted them unconditionally. Instead, I foolishly squandered away those gifts in my efforts to protect you."

Sam could tell how sincere and sorry his father was for how he had treated him. Sam said nothing; he just sat down next to him and placed his hand on his father's shoulder.

After several minutes passed by, Sam asked his father, "Where did this power come from Dad? What has Padre Pio have to do with Grandpa and me?"

"When your grandfather came home from the war, he was a different person. He piloted B-17 bombers during the war from '43-'45 and spent most of the war flying out of airbases in Italy. He was sent there when U.S. forces invaded mainland Italy in '43. I remember going to the movies every Saturday and watching the newsreels that showed the brutal fighting that was going there as the Allies tried to push the Germans out of Italy. It showed footage of U.S. troops landing at Salerno, fighting at Monte Cassino, Anzio—all those different places. They talked about the cold, the mountainous terrain, the German artillery—it was a terrible. One time they showed a B-17 being attacked by German fighters, and it was literally shot in half, folded up upon itself, and then broke into hundreds of pieces. I kept picturing my father inside being torn to pieces. My mother never told me exactly where he was stationed, but I can remember eavesdropping on her when she was talking to other people. She mentioned all the places in Italy that I saw in the newsreels. I prayed every night for my father to come home alive.

After the German's surrendered and the fighting ended in Europe, fathers, sons, brothers, and uncles from the neighborhood started coming home. At first, everyone from the neighborhood would go to their houses to welcome them home. Then as more came home; some severely wounded and some with combat fatigue, we started giving people more privacy. My father was one of the last in the neighborhood to come home, and I remember being petrified at the thought of seeing him. I didn't know if he was going to come home with a missing arm, leg, or even crippled. Just as frightening was the thought of him being psychologically wounded. My neighbor who was a few years older than me told me about his brother. He said his brother would have terror dreams almost every night, and during the day I could see him in the backyard just staring into space. They called it the thousand-yard stare back then. Some of the others would have these terrible tremors and become startled at the slightest of noises. It was so hard to see, and all I could think about was that was going to be my father when he came home.

Then, one day, I heard the front door open, and my mother screaming that my father was home. Instead of running, I slowly and apprehensively walked out of my room and down the stairs afraid to even look at him. I didn't look at him until I was on the very last step of the stairway. When I finally looked up at him—all my fears melted away. I will never forget the look on his face. His face was glowing. He didn't look withdrawn and weak like the other soldiers returning home. Calmness and tranquility seemed to emanate from every fiber of his being. I remember hugging him so hard and him hugging me back. When we pulled away from each other he looked at me and said, 'Everything is okay now son—I'm home.' Looking at him then, I knew that this was not the same person who left us two years ago. *Something* happened overseas that changed him forever, because he seemed to be at total peace with himself and the world."

"What happened to him in Italy, Dad?" Sam asked.

"Listen … I know some horrible things happened there and I could tell that he didn't want to discuss them with me. He just didn't want to upset me. However, I know it was bad because some nights I would hear him softly crying in his room. As time passed though, he started sharing a few stories here and there, but they were always positive—mostly stories about the friends he made in the war. For the longest time, he never really talked about the missions that he went on. Maybe he didn't want to think about all the soldiers and civilians that were killed by the bombs he dropped. I don't know for sure."

"Then, one fall day we were in the backyard raking leaves together. I remember the day clearly; it was crisp, cold, and really sunny. We had several huge maples in the backyard, and it looked like there was an ocean of leaves on the ground. Within a half hour my father and I were shedding layers of clothes from working so hard. When we were about three-quarters of the way done and surrounded by the mountains of leaves that we had raked up, I finally said to him, Dad, how come you didn't come home from the war like so many of the others in our neighborhood?"

"What do you mean Anthony?" he said to me.

"I said, 'You know—a lot of the guys came back kinda … messed up.'"

"He turned to me and said, 'Son, I could have easily ended up just like them—maybe even worse.'"

"But why didn't you Dad" I said. "I mean you seemed so different from when you left for the war. You seemed so calm, even happy when you came back from the war. Why didn't you end up like them?"

"My father didn't answer right away. He just stood there, shifting his weight back and forth onto the handle of the rake, all the while staring at the ground. Then he looked up and said, 'I guess God decided to change his plans for me, son.'"

Chapter 45

Sam got up from the trunk and pulled up a chair in front of his father and said, "Did he tell you why he felt God changed the direction of his life?

Sam's father continued, "At the time, your grandfather could tell by my expression that I didn't understand what he meant and desperately wanted to know more. I could tell he didn't want to go any further, but fortunately, he did."

"'Let me tell you something Anthony...' your grandfather said. 'When I left for the war, I thought I had everything figured out. The world to me was black and white—there was no gray. I knew what I wanted in life, I knew what was right and wrong, and those that didn't think the same way I thought were fools. My view was that each person made his or her life; it wasn't thrust upon you by fate or God. If things weren't going your way, it was your fault, and you had to fix it. My mother always told me that I needed to stop being so rigid in my thinking and be more open to the ideas of others. She continually stressed to me the idea of having faith in God and the role he played in our lives. Now, I believed in the idea of a God at the time, but I felt I could take care of my own life, and didn't need a God to intercede or guide me. When I was sent overseas during the war, a lot of the guys would pray before missions, but I just didn't see the need. If I didn't make it back, it would be because a mistake was made by either me or my crew, not because God decided to take us.'"

"Then your grandfather stopped for a second, and stood their kind of laughing at himself. He said, 'Of course that was until I met a person during the war that basically shattered all my views on life and God forever.'"

"I asked him, who? Who did you meet Dad? He didn't answer right away. He simply reached into his back pocket and pulled out a small photo from his wallet."

Sam interrupted his father, "You mean—the picture of him with Padre Pio?"

"Yes, that same picture Sam," his father replied.

Adrenaline raced through Sam's body; all the lifelong questions and doubts were about to be unraveled. Sam said, "Dad, what did Grandpa say about Padre Pio? How did they meet?"

Mr. Amonte looked intently at Sam and said, "Son, I know that you are looking to me to answer all your questions. I know that you desperately want to know how this gift of healing came to you, but I will never be able to answer all your questions. I simply do not understand it all myself. Your grandfather never shared the entire story with me. He said that he couldn't because it was between God and himself."

Sam pleaded with his father, "He had to have shared something Dad! Did he say anything else?"

Mr. Amonte replied, "He did, but you have to understand, it will not give you the answers to all your questions."

"Anything Dad. Please give me something to hold on to. I need to know something more," Sam pleaded. Mr. Amonte continued, "On that fall day, I begged your grandfather to tell me more about the person in the photo. He said it would be too difficult for me to understand, and he wasn't really sure if he completely understood it either. I said to him, Dad, I'm almost a teenager now. I was the man of the house when you were gone. I took care of mom. Please tell me."

"I think me saying that convinced him, because your grandfather looked at me and said, 'You did a great job as the man of the house Anthony—you stepped up when I needed you most.'"

"Right after that he shared this story with me ..." "Towards the end of his tour of duty, his outfit, the 2nd Bomber Group, was sent to the Amendola Airbase in Italy. They were flying missions out of this base and relentlessly bombing the German troops dug in in northern Italy. The U.S. planes were decimating their front lines, but at the same time they were losing a lot of men as well. One evening, they were flying back to base after a night raid when the B-17 your grandfather was piloting began to start losing altitude fast. He did everything he could to keep altitude, but he could not stop the plane from going down. He had a crew of nine other men on the plane that night. He told them to parachute out, but it was too late. They were way off course and going down too fast. The last thing he remembered before crashing was pulling back on the yoke with all his strength and hearing the sound of the plane tearing apart and terrifying screams. Then he said everything went black. That was until he saw a bright light in the distance. As he approached the light, an all-encompassing sense of peace overtook his mind and body. The force and attraction of this light beckoned him and he said he could not resist. As he drew closer to the light, he felt a presence behind him and then a grasp of his hand. He looked back and saw a man. This man looked at him and said, 'It is not your time Anthony. There is more for you to do.'

The next thing that he remembered was waking up in a hospital at Foggia Airbase, but he wasn't severely wounded, just a few minor cuts and scrapes. But his crew … they had all been killed. No one could figure out how he survived a crash like that with such minor injuries. When he was released from the hospital a few days later, he was given a week's leave. He didn't want to leave Italy, so he hitched a few rides and visited a few towns within a couple hundred miles of the base. He felt the slow pace of life in these small Italian villages was just what he needed. He needed time to think about what had happened to him. He needed so many questions answered. Why was he the only one to survive? Why was he given a second chance? Who was the man who spoke to him after the crash? What was left for him to do in life? After six days of traveling, he wasn't any closer to answering these questions.

Then on the seventh day, he reached a town called San Giovanni Rotundo. As he walked past a small chapel in the town, he felt the sudden urge to go in. He had not been to church in many years, but for some reason he felt he needed to go in. When he walked into the chapel, he noticed a few people praying, so he sat down in the last pew of the church and did something that he hadn't done since his confirmation—he prayed. He said he prayed for the souls of each one of his crewmembers and asked God to help him to understand why he alone had been spared. Although he left with no answers, he felt more at peace.

On his way out of the church, he opened the chapel doors and bright sunshine temporarily blinded him as he walked out into the street. While trying to shield his eyes from the sun, he bumped into a man in a robe who seemed to be a monk from the nearby monastery. He said to him, 'Please excuse me Father, I am sorry.'

Due to the sun and the fact that the monk's head was bowed down, he could not see the monk's face. However, the monk did reach his hand out and touch your grandfather's hand. He noticed that the monk's hand had a glove on it with the fingers cut out. Then the monk spoke to him and said, 'No need ... you are forgiven my son. Go forth, and do God's will.'

Your grandfather just stood there in the street and watched him slowly walk away from him. The monk's voice and touch seemed so familiar to your grandfather, but he did not know why.

The next day, he was eating breakfast at a café that had quite a few other servicemen there. While he was sipping coffee, he noticed a boy going around to some of the tables of the servicemen trying to sell them photographs. Apparently, the day before, this young boy had followed some of the soldiers around and had taken candid pictures of them at various points around town. A lot of the servicemen were appreciative of the photos and bought them from the boy. The guys at the table next to him were laughing at some of the photos when the boy came up to your grandfather and put a photo on his table. The boy said in broken English, 'You buy ... uno dollar?' When your grandfather looked down at the picture, he realized it was a photo of him and the monk in front of the chapel from the day before. The boy then pointed to the photo and said, 'You … Padre Pio.' and then knelt down and made the sign of the cross.

Your grandfather paid and thanked him, then picked up the picture and noticed that he could clearly see the monk's face. When he saw his face, he realized immediately that the monk he had bumped into in front of the chapel was the same man who led him away from the light after the plane crash. Sam … Padre Pio was the one who saved your grandfather's life."

Chapter 46

"There is still one thing that I don't understand Dad", Sam said to his father. "Why did you resent Grandpa so much for having this power to heal, and why did you feel it was so important to protect me from it?"

"Listen Sam, my father *embraced* his power. He saw it as a gift and never shied away from it for one minute. He saw it as an opportunity to spread love and happiness to people to ease their pain and suffering. However, there is usually a hidden cost to everything in life, even the positive. While he eased the burdens of many people with his power to heal, it only added to the burdens of our family."

"What happened to your family?" Sam asked.

"One of the toughest things for me growing up was the fact that we could never stay in one place for very long. We would move into a new town, I would start to make new friends, get used to the new school, and then my father would become the talk of the town, the talk of county, the talk of the state. News would travel fast about his ability to heal. Soon people would start showing up at our house looking for his help. However, for every person that loved and believed in him, twenty despised him. In some cases, they even wanted to see him dead. There were so many times in my childhood where I went to bed with the fear that my father or family would be killed.

This fear became so commonplace that I became very good at recognizing the people who could be a threat to my family. They were what I would call the "angry and the righteous". They always proclaimed themselves to have a special relationship with God; the most "righteous" and "moral" people in the town. They had the outward appearance of being devout and religious, but I could always detect the anger and contempt in their hearts.

Why do you think I showed up at the school board meeting that night Sam? I knew he was a threat to you that night. You probably don't remember this, but when you saved Jimmy, an article appeared in the paper the next day. In the article, there were quotes from several people, and the one that always stuck in my mind was the one from our neighbor Jim Flanigan. I never forgot what he said. He said that you were 'an affront to the Lord Our Savior' and will have to 'answer to the Lord someday'. Whenever I heard words like that said about my father growing up, I knew I had to protect my family from those people.

When the news stories started appearing about you in the newspaper recently, everyone around town began talking about it. One night, I heard Flanigan shooting his mouth off at the VFW Post. He had been drinking heavily, and a story about you came on the television. His comments on that night immediately propelled me back to my childhood. He used the very same words that I had heard so many times growing up about my father. I made it a point to go to the VFW over the next several nights to watch him. When another story came on about you announcing the date of the board of education meeting, I saw that look in his eye. It was a mixture of contempt, anger and hate.

I followed Flanigan the entire day of the board meeting. When I saw him get on the thruway, I knew he was going there to hurt you. I shadowed him throughout the entire meeting, staying just behind him, so he would not spot me. When the meeting ended and the crowd started moving out of the building, I temporarily lost him and panicked. At the last minute, I saw him from across the crowd slowly making his way towards you. I almost didn't make it in time. Thank God, I don't know what I would have done if he would have ..."

Sam put his hand on his father's shoulder and said, "But he didn't. You saved me Dad."

Mr. Amonte smiled wryly at those words, for he knew that he would not have survived the shooting if his son was not able to make it to the hospital that night.

Chapter 47

After the shooting, Sam did not arrive at the hospital that night for nearly two hours. Due to the chaos that ensued at the board meeting, the police did not allow Sam to leave their custody until they could determine the exact series of events that occurred. At least he managed to tell Angelina to follow the ambulance to the hospital. Sam was frantic by the time he finally reached the hospital.

When Sam entered the trauma unit, he saw Angelina standing outside an operating room with his mother and a physician. At first, Sam was taken aback at the sight of his mother. His mother looked so much older. It was at this point that he had realized just how long it had been since he had last seen her. His mother turned to Angelina and buried her head into Angelina's shoulder sobbing. Angelina was embracing her and tears began rolling down her cheeks. His worst fears were playing out before his eyes.

When Angelina and his mother spotted him coming down the hallway, his mother rushed towards him and threw her arms around him. She held him with such force that it took Sam's breath away. Sam hugged her closely and struggled to speak. He tried hard to pull himself together, and was finally able to speak.

"Ma, is he dead?"

His mother looked down and nodded her head confirming his worst fears.

"When?" he asked.

"About an hour ago, Sam." she replied.

"Where is he Mom?" he asked his mother.

She looked away from his glance and said, "He is in the operating room down the hall."

Just then, his mother looked up at him with an expression of desperation.

"Son … you can help him?"

"Ma, I don't … I mean … It has been too long … I don't know."

"Please Sam—you have to try!" she pleaded.

Mrs. Amonte stared up at her son and saw a look of indecisiveness and despair transform into a look of determination. Sam turned to the doctor and said, "Where is my father?"

The doctor replied, "He is Operating Room C, but son, you don't want to go in there right now his body will not be prepared for you to…"

Sam was already halfway down the hall before the doctor could finish speaking.

When Sam entered the operating room, an aide was inside cleaning up his father's blood soak clothes, gauze pads, and instruments. His father's body was covered with a sheet.

The orderly asked him who he was, and Sam explained that the man on the table was his father. The orderly told him that he was sorry for Sam's loss and said that he would come back a little later to finish cleaning.

Sam stood next to the table staring at the outline of his father's body under the sheet. He was afraid to lift the sheet and see his father's lifeless face, so he stood there for a few moments trying to prepare himself. After one long deep breath, he slowly pulled the sheet from his father's face.

Sam reached down, touched his face and said, "Dad … Oh Dad … I am so sorry."

He looked so old to Sam. The passage of time had not been kind to his father. He knew he had been away for a very long time, but he was still shocked by the lines and wrinkles on his father's face. It was at this point that he realized what a mistake it had been to leave his family. Sam fought to push those thoughts from his mind—he had to stay focused on what needed to be done.

Even though Sam had healed others before, he had never been in a situation like this. Yes, he had brought Jimmy back to life, but Jimmy was only dead for a short period of time—his body wasn't even cold yet when he brought him back to life in the ambulance. His father, on the other hand, had been dead for over an hour and had severe damage to his vital organs and tissue. Fear and doubt overtook him in the operating room, and the assuredness and confidence he felt in previous healings was absent.

Scenes from his life raced through his mind; the deer smashing into the windshield, Jimmy lying by the side of the pitching mound, his father punching the news reporter, his mother and father fighting, his father silently sitting at the kitchen table as he left his life behind—the room began to spin until Sam fell to his knees. His mind and body felt paralyzed.

Then Sam did something that he had never done before a healing—he prayed. Still on his knees, he clasped his hands together and rested his head against the side of the surgical table. As he knelt there, he did not know what to say; it had been so long since he had prayed that he felt guilty. "How do I even start?" he thought to himself. It was then that he remembered something. Sam reached into his back pocket and opened his wallet. From his wallet he pulled out a small laminated card—the prayer card that Margarita Sanchez gave him the night in the hospital when he healed her granddaughter. He had not looked at it since that night, yet for some reason he always kept it with him. Putting all thoughts out of his mind—the shooting, his past, his regrets, everything, he stared at the picture of Padre Pio. Soon his heart and mind began to calm and the words came to him.

"Dear Lord...you're a mystery to me. I know that I haven't always been faithful in my life. I know I've closed myself off to you. I haven't been a faithful servant and for that I'm truly sorry. I wouldn't blame you for ignoring my pleas right now, and I know that I am not deserving of your mercy, but there must be a reason why you have bestowed this gift of upon me ..."

Sam had finally said it. It was a <u>gift</u>—it wasn't the curse that had ruined his life.

198

Then Sam turned over the prayer card and began to recite the prayer: "*Dear God, You generously blessed Your servant, St. Pio of Pietrelcina, with the gifts of the Spirit. You marked his body with the five wounds of Christ Crucified, as a powerful witness to the saving Passion and Death of Your Son ...Through the intercession of St. Pio of Pietrelcina, I confidently beseech You to grant me the grace of helping me to heal my father and bring him to back life. Glory be to the Father and to the Son and to the Holy Spirit, as it was in the beginning, is now and ever shall be, World without end. Amen*"

Sam repeated this prayer over and over again until confidence, humility, and compassion began to overwhelm his feelings of guilt and doubt.

It was then that Sam felt the light touch of hands upon his shoulders. He had felt that gentle touch many times before; it was the old man again. Immediately a wave of peacefulness coursed through his body, making his mind, body, and soul feel lighter. The old man gently supported him by the elbows and lifted him to his feet. Just as Sam was about to turn and speak to him, the man grabbed his hands and placed them on his father's face. Sam looked down at the man's hands and saw that they had deep wounds in them—the same exact wounds that he had suffered after healing Paige.

As the warm, bright light engulfed the room, Sam felt his father's face begin to warm and saw its' bluish tone begin to change to the rosy hue of life.

Chapter 48

For the first time in many years, Sam had the opportunity to spend a considerable amount of time with his family. With the school year over, Angelina was able to join him in his visits. With each visit, Angelina and his parents became closer and closer. His parents clearly loved Angelina, and she them. The affection they felt towards one another was effortless. However, for Sam and his father, it was much more complicated.

Sam knew his father regretted turning his back on Sam for possessing a gift that he neither understood nor asked for. Sam could see it in his father's eyes whenever they talked about the past. Sam reassured his father frequently that he needed to put the past behind him, and try to concentrate more on the future. One day, when he saw that look of regret and anguish in his father's eyes during a conversation, Sam said to him, "Dad, think about what happened on the day of the shooting. Do you think that God planned for you to take a bullet for me, and gave me the grace to save you, so we could dwell on the past for the rest of our lives? The events that occurred on that day were presented to us as an opportunity to focus on the future—not to relive the past."

As much as Sam meant that, he and his father realized that they had a challenge ahead—they had to renew their relationship from scratch. So, during the warm summer months of that year, they spent most of the time together simply trying to get to know one another again. Both men had changed considerably over the years. To Sam, this was clearly not the same man who watched him walk out the kitchen door at the age of eighteen. His father seemed kinder and gentler. As the weeks passed by, for the first time in his life, he was able to see the man his grandmother and mother saw all those years. On those special visits of his youth to his grandmother's house, Sam witnessed the moments of the tenderness and love between his father and grandmother. But, because they were so fleeting and infrequent, the only thing Sam really remembered about his father were his frequent displays of detachment and resentment. During that summer, his father had turned those memories upside down. The wall that had existed between him and his father was no longer there. His father's frequent acts of understanding, compassion, and love turned that wall to dust.

To Mr. Amonte, Sam had become a man. However, not just any man, a man that he truly admired. His son went out into the world at eighteen; supported himself, earned a Master's degree, and decided to devote his life to help secure the dreams and aspirations of the next generation of children. Any parent would be proud of this, but Sam achieved all this with the added burden of trying to navigate through the emotional minefield that came with his power to heal. Mr. Amonte knew what that minefield was like. He watched his own father navigate the blasts and upheavals of this minefield throughout his whole life. However, there was one difference between his son and his father, and it was this difference that he admired most about Sam; his father had a loving spouse by his side during this incredible journey and Sam had walked the majority of it alone. Now that he had his son back, Mr. Amonte wasn't going to let him to walk it alone anymore.

One hot summer day, Sam and his father were sitting on the porch together watching the rain come down. They sat there in silence for nearly an hour overtaken by the tranquility of the sights, sounds, and smells of the rain until Mr. Amonte broke the silence,

"Son ... Have you thought about when you are going to go back to teaching?"

Sam thought about the question for a moment and said, "Dad, I am not sure I am going to be able to teach again."

"What do you mean?" his father replied, "Your teaching license was not taken away. You can find another job son."

"Dad, you have to understand," Sam said, "No, they didn't take away my license, but who is going to take a chance on someone who was the center of such controversy? Even if they didn't see all of this play out on the news, they are ultimately going to ask why I had to leave my last job, and background checks will be made. I may have to look at doing something else with my life."

Mr. Amonte rocked in his chair for a few moments then turned to Sam and said, "Sam, I am going to say the same thing to you that you said to me not very long ago. Do you think God meant for all this to happen so that you could become a lawyer, mechanic, or accountant? You weren't just given one special gift, you were given two, and the other is your ability to teach. Son, you can't give up on that. Do you think Jimmy would have wanted you to do that?"

Sam realized that his father was right. He loved teaching and if it was meant to be, he would find a job again. However, he needed to get out there and see if it was possible. Even though he and Angelina had moved out of the Cayuga district, she was still employed there. He hoped to find a job somewhere in the area, however, he knew that it was not going to be easy. He hoped that enough time had passed for people to forget about him and the incident, but he wouldn't know for sure until he got out there to interview. He felt the best place to start would be to attend the Teacher Recruitment Job Fair at the downtown convention center. Hopefully, some of the recruiters would not recognize, or remember him as the center of controversy several months ago.

When he arrived at the job fair, he saw a huge ballroom filled with school districts from all over the state. Just the sheer volume of recruiters in the room lifted his spirits and gave him hope. For the next several hours, Sam introduced himself to at least fifteen different recruiters. He started each conversation talking about his vast teaching experiences, and most recruiters seemed very impressed by his experience, personal qualities, and skills. Yet, when it came time for him to pass along his resume, and they noticed that his last job was in the Cayuga District, they suddenly seemed less interested. Sam realized that he was wrong; enough time had not passed, and no one was going to take a chance on him. In fact, by the end of the day, after speaking to twenty-five different recruiters, only *one* school district showed any interest in him—a small parochial high school about 80 miles away.

Feeling tired and dejected, Sam started to make his way towards the door when he heard a voice calling from the distance, "Mr. Amonte! Sam!"

Sam turned around, but could not see who was calling him through the crowd. He continued to scan the room until he spotted a person waving to him from a small table in the corner of the ballroom. The banner on the small table read, "*Cayuga Central*" and the person calling his name was Mr. Massina.

Sam waved to him and slowly walked over to his table. Mr. Massina walked out from behind the table, reached his hand out and said, "Sam, how are you? It is so good to see you."

Sam shook his hand and replied, "It is good to see you as well, Mr. Massina."

"I see that you are getting back in the job market. That is great Sam. Have you had any luck today?"

Sam did not want Mr. Massina to know how discouraged he was so he replied, "Not too bad. I think I have one strong lead—a small school district just down the thruway."

Mr. Massina could tell that things had not gone well for Sam that day, and tried to cheer him up.

"You are a talented teacher Sam. You belong in this profession. You have to be positive and have faith in yourself."

"Thanks Mr. Massina," Sam said. "I appreciate your words of encouragement. You have always been supportive of me. I know what you tried to do for me at Cayuga, and I will never forget that. Listen, again, it has been great to see you, but I think I am going to head out now. I wish you all the best Mr. Massina."

Sam extended his hand, and Mr. Massina clutched it tightly and said, "You're a good man Sam. I will always be proud of the fact that you worked at my school."

Sam acknowledged Mr. Massina's kind words with a simple nod of his head and walked away.

When Sam arrived home, Angelina had a wonderful dinner ready on the table, and had opened an expensive bottle of wine.

"How did it go today, honey?" she said.

"It went okay. I think I may have a shot at a position in a parochial high school not too far from here. It would be a little bit of a commute, but not too bad."

"That's great! Did they say when they would contact you?"

"They didn't say, Angie."

Angelina walked up to Sam, grabbed his hands and said, "What's wrong? You don't seem too excited."

"Angie, I talked to twenty-five recruiters today and had only *one* lead. People are not going to come near me around here. I guess I was just kidding myself thinking that I could get back in the classroom."

"Sam, you have to give it a little more time." she said.

"Maybe … But I have to be realistic too. Listen, I am not saying that I regret anything that happened, or that I am feeling sorry for myself, but I want a future for us Angie. I don't want to waste several years on something that is not going to happen. I want to marry you, and I can't do that without a good job."

Sam looked at Angelina, and watched the corners of her mouth slowly curl up into a sly smile. She placed her hands warmly around the back of his neck, pulled him close, and said, "What did you say you wanted to do? Did you say that you wanted to *marry* me?"

Sam smiled back at her, picked her up off the floor into his arms and said, "No, no. I didn't say marry, I said I wanted to *carry* you. Sam picked her up from the kitchen and brought her into the living room and set her down playfully onto the couch.

"See," he said, "*Carry* you."

Angelina pulled him by the waist on top of her and pressed her lips to his. When Sam pulled away to momentarily smile at her, Angelina quickly and forcefully pulled him back to her until she felt his body fully surrender to her passionate and loving embrace. As Angelina pulled her lips from Sam's, she stared into his eyes and self-assuredly said, "You know you want to marry me."

Before he could reply, she flashed a blithe smile and tauntingly said, "Admit it! Admit it! You want to marry me!"

Sam replied, "Yeah, maybe I'll keep you around a little longer."

When the telephone rang, Angelina begged him not to answer it. Sam promised he would come right back and finished what he started.

Sam answered the telephone, "Hello …"

"Yes, this is Sam …"

"How are you …?"

"It was nice to talk to you today as well …"

"Tomorrow? Absolutely! …"

 "I will look forward to it."

Sam hung up the phone, looked at Angelina and said, "I've got an interview!"

Chapter 49

It was the first day of school, and Sam could feel the butterflies in his stomach. He had not felt like this on the first day of school for many years. Even though he had experienced this countless times before, he could not stop himself from feeling nervous.

He had arrived at school early that morning to put some finishing touches on his room—hanging a few more posters, arranging the desks, and dragging in a comfy recliner for the kids. He had his seating charts all laid out for each class, and went over some of the more challenging student names on the class rosters. He did not like to mispronounce student names on the first day.

About fifteen minutes before his first students arrived, he heard his cell phone vibrating on his desk signaling that a text had just been sent. He picked up his phone, and it was a text from Angelina that said, *"Good luck today, honey—I love you!"* Sam smiled and felt more relaxed.

When the bell rang signaling the end of homeroom, Sam went out into the hallway to meet his first class. He watched students as they poured out of their homerooms and into the hallways. It was a frenzy of activity; kids catching up with each other about what went on over the summer, comparing new outfits, seeing who was in whose class, and checking and re-checking their schedules.

As his first students came towards his room, he straightened his tie and adjusted his jacket.

"Am I in the right class?" one female student said.

Sam looked at her schedule and replied, "Why, yes you are, and what is your name young lady?"

"Stop it, you know who I am?" she said.

"Let's see," he said reading her schedule. "Is it Oliver Pinchpot?"

"Ha-Ha, she said. It's O-l-i-v-i-a, Olivia *Pinchot*."

"Oh yeah, I think I remember you," he said with a smile.

The next student walked up and said, "Still no ring on that finger, huh Mr. A? You better get on that soon or some social studies teacher I know is going to leave you for a good looking phys. ed. teacher."

"Listen, Daequan," said Sam. "I am not worried about any phys. ed. teacher. Now get your tail in class."

Daequan shot him back a big smile.

The next student came up from behind and gave him a big hug. "Mr. A! Oh my God! I knew you would be back!"

He replied, "It is good to be back Alexandra."

The next sound he heard startled him for a second, but at the same instantly warmed his heart—the beep of a horn.

When he turned around, he looked down to see Andrew in his wheelchair with a huge smile on his face. Andrew looked up at him and said, "Are you going to stand out in the hallway all day, or are you going to teach us?"

Andrew beeped his horn again, and Sam stepped aside, bowed, and motioned his arm towards the door.

"After you, Mr. Lambert."

Once he was certain that all his students had arrived, he took a deep breath and walked through the doorway of his classroom. Just before he closed the door, he heard his name being called from the hallway. He opened the door up again and stepped outside his room to see who was calling him. When he looked to his left, he saw Mr. Lohrman standing in the hallway alone. Mr. Lohrman extended his hand out to Sam and said,

"I just wanted to come by and wish you the best of luck this year."

Sam shook his hand and said,

"I don't know how I can ever thank you for giving me this opportunity again, Mr. Lohrman. I couldn't believe it when Mr. Massina called me to set up an interview. I know this had to be an extremely difficult decision for you. I still don't know how you convinced the school board to give me a second chance. Why would they risk the public scrutiny? There are so many good teachers out there ..."

Mr. Lohrman cut Sam off in mid-sentence, "You are right. There are a lot of good teachers out there. But how many are truly great? You risked everything in your life for one individual student who sat in the second row of your class. One student, amongst thousands, you have probably taught in your career. I don't think I will ever understand *why* or *how* you did what you did, however, I know it is not *you* who should be thanking *me*. I will never be able to repay you for what you did for not only my daughter, but for my whole family. I was blinded by the love I had for my wife. Looking back, I know there were signs, but it was just incomprehensible to me that she could ever hurt Paige. My wife was just never the same after Emily's death and her two deployments in the Middle East. But she is getting the help she needs now, and we are slowly picking up the pieces of our life again. We have a chance now. Believe me Sam; the risk the school board has taken is inconsequential compared to the risk you took for my daughter."

With those last words, Mr. Lohrman turned and walked down the hallway away from Sam's room. When he heard Sam enter his room and close the door, the sound of cheers could be heard echoing down the hallway.

Mr. Lohrman stopped, listened for a moment, then smiled and kept on walking.

www.ingramcontent.com/pod-product-compliance
Lightning Source LLC
Chambersburg PA
CBHW070838120626
46556CB00002B/790